What a pair they were—both wounded and wrapped in the past.

O God, help us.

Laura had heard the thunder of his heart when Eli pulled her close. Uncertainty? Yearning? His gentleness as he stroked her shoulder suggested the latter, but right now she wanted only his friendship. She needed more time to heal.

Eli pulled his hat brim down and stood. "I want to ride over the ridge behind the ranch before we head back. You game?"

She gathered the remains of their breakfast. "I'm game."

Eli offered her a hand and pulled her up, sweeping her face with a blue gaze. She squeezed his fingers before releasing her grip, but he held on.

She aimed for a lighthearted tone, but it snagged in her throat.

"What is it?"

"I'm glad you came back," he said softly.

DAVALYNN SPENCER'S

love of writing has taken her from the national rodeo circuit and a newsroom's daily crime beat to college classrooms and inspirational publications. When not writing romance or teaching, she speaks at women's retreats and plays on her church's worship team. She and her husband have three children and four grandchildren and make their home on Colorado's Front Range with a Queensland heeler named Blue. To learn more about Davalynn visit her website at www.davalynnspencer.com.

DAVALYNN SPENCER

The Rancher's Second Chance

HEARTSONG
PRESENTS

Recycling programs
for this product may
not exist in your area.

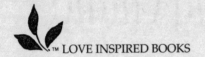

™ LOVE INSPIRED BOOKS

ISBN-13: 978-0-373-48671-7

THE RANCHER'S SECOND CHANCE

Copyright © 2013 by Davalynn Spencer

www.LoveInspiredBooks.com

Printed in U.S.A.

Behold, I make all things new.
    —*Revelation* 21:5

For all who think their wounds
are beyond God's healing reach.

Chapter 1

Laura Bell geared down and turned left on the county road. Faded asphalt stretched out long and lean past Hawthorne Ranch and up into the foothills, threading a tight S-curve at the top of a small rise. Her Mercedes SLK-350 hugged the twisting roadway like a close friend.

Across from a tight row of mailboxes she hooked a sharp right at a private lane, slid to a stop and waited for the dust to settle. That's when she saw him—reined in near a scrub oak cluster, as if waiting for her to get out of the way.

Wonderful. An audience.

Defensive about her stirring arrival, she pulled the emergency brake, stepped out of the convertible and yanked at her black pencil skirt.

The cowboy leaned forward, arms crossed on his saddle horn, reins hanging loosely from his fingers. A wide-brimmed hat hid his eyes.

His shoulders bounced once, as if he'd laughed and held it inside.

She pushed her sunglasses tight against her face and raised her chin. He may not know it yet, but he did not want to laugh at her.

Ignoring him, she spiked her way through the weeds in four-inch heels toward a Realtor's For Sale sign. Wrapping one perfectly manicured hand around each side, she jerked upward, but it wouldn't give. She pushed against it with her hip and tried again.

Frustrated, and feeling as graceful as an elephant on ice, she bent the sign back and forth, hoping to loosen the stakes. She tugged again. Not a budge.

A leathery squeak drew her gaze around to see the cowboy stepping from his saddle. Three long strides brought him to the sign, and with a hand firmly gripped around each stake, he pulled.

Nothing.

Privately pleased that the Lone Ranger couldn't get the sign out either, Laura folded her arms across her pink silk blouse and angled one open-toe stiletto in front of the other.

He continued to pull. No lunging or pushing, just a steady upward tug that flexed the muscles in his tanned forearms. She could imagine what his biceps looked like at the moment.

The sign surrendered. The cowboy pulled it free of the earth, and handed it to her with a sober look. A black patch covered one eye.

She took the surprisingly heavy sign and looked away. "Thank you."

In her hurry to leave, she spun on one foot. The thin heel snapped off, and she tilted dangerously to the right.

He caught her by the arm and held on until she regained her balance.

"Thanks," she mumbled.

"No problem."

She detected a humorous note in his voice and tightened her grip on the sign.

Limping to her car, she leaned over the driver's door,

reached under the steering wheel and popped the trunk. Then she laid the sign in the back, took off her ruined shoes and tossed them in.

Roadside grit stuck between her toes.

A quick glance revealed the cowboy standing next to his horse, thumbs hooked in his jeans and an odd tilt to his mouth. Something seemed familiar.

Too embarrassed to acknowledge him further, she slid behind the wheel, released the brake and eyed the lane that looped up and around the hill. That narrow climb had been the road home for the first twelve years of her life. The best years.

The past twelve? Not so much.

Unaccustomed to driving barefoot, she misjudged the clutch, the car lurched forward and the engine died.

Heat burned her ears and neck and she hoped her silent observer couldn't see the blush from where he stood. She tried again, and successfully shifted through first and into second for the half-mile climb.

The horseman disappeared from her rearview mirror on the first curve, and at the top she parked next to the house, shut off the engine and stared.

Memory had failed her.

Hawthorne pastures spread across the valley like a rumpled green quilt. Oak trees and granite boulders knotted the landscape, and red pipe fences still trimmed the ranch. Black angus cattle grazed. And just east of the center of it all, just east of the Hawthorne's ranch house and barns, the guest house and lawns, lay the pond—a gray-blue jewel. Canada geese squatted along the western edge and mallards paddled under the shady arms of an overhanging oak.

Peace.

She stepped out of the car and blinked away the mist in her eyes. Standing barefoot at the edge of the steep slope, she breathed in the summery perfume of wild grass and oak leaves. Her throat tightened at the memories and the tragic possibilities of *what-if.*

What if the place had sold?

These twenty acres of hill and lowland that bordered the beautiful Hawthorne Ranch were all she had left of her family, of the good years. She was suddenly grateful for California's slumping real estate market. Selling could have been a horrible mistake. As horrible as marrying Derek Stone.

Laura sat on the granite edge, not caring whether her skirt snagged. So be it. She didn't plan to wear it again anyway. It belonged to a life she'd left behind forever, a life of Derek's reshaping, designed to fit into his metropolitan mold.

Insisting his fiancée drive a new Mercedes, he'd let her choose his engagement gift, though he grimaced at her preference for the steel-blue roadster.

Now, gazing down at the beautiful, peaceful reason, she felt vindicated.

She pulled off her sunglasses, took the pins from her hair and shook its length down her back.

Derek had insisted on other things, too, and she'd foolishly agreed just to please him. She'd changed the way she dressed, the way she wore her hair, her job. And she'd given up her dream of a wedding in the Spring Valley Chapel.

Too country, he'd said.

Her heritage didn't fit his lifestyle, and he'd shown little interest in her past.

Unfortunately, she hadn't shown enough in his, or she might have noticed the warning signs earlier.

And then Mama died.

The decision to bring her mother's body home to be buried next to Daddy had opened Laura's eyes to a future she didn't have. Why not move back home? At least for a year. She could live that long on the life insurance policy, substitute at the local school, get her bearings.

She scheduled the funeral, took the property off the market, packed her personal belongings and left.

A movement caught her eye and pulled her back to the present. The mysterious rider made his way along the road, onto the ranch and straight to a corner gate where he sidled up next to it and swung it open without dismounting. Hinges moaned as he closed the gate on his way through.

Quite a hand, she grudgingly admitted.

Leaving the view for later, she gathered her few things from the car and fingered through her key ring. The lock on the house had never been changed, even during the early years when Mama rented it out for extra income. She inserted the key, turned the knob and stepped back in time as she stepped through the double French doors and into a wall of stale, mousy air.

No surprise. Emptiness did that to a house. Dust covered the kitchen counters and what little furniture remained. Clean square poison boxes lay scattered about, evidence that at least one rodent generation had perished. But others had come. It was the country, after all. She'd get a cat.

She set her bags in the corner of her parents' old room and then turned in a slow circle.

She'd bought a sleeping bag, but it wouldn't do, not with the mice. She'd have to spring for a real bed.

At the window, an overgrown mulberry tree blocked her view of the pond and ranch. She toured the other two bedrooms, walked through the dining room and living room, and out onto the covered front porch that stretched the length of the house.

Below her a dog barked and a smile seamed her lips as she remembered the Hawthornes' golden retriever pup. Memories rushed in and pulled her down the ranch lane that led to the pond and picnic area. She had run there with Eli Hawthorne III and his dog, pumping her short legs to keep up with Eli's longer strides. He ran with two fishing poles and a tackle box, and still he beat her to the pond, claiming the best spot beneath the tree.

Annoyance niggled into the memory. Sometimes she'd resented Eli's arrogance and dominating attitude. And sometimes she worshipped him.

She'd heard whispers at her mother's funeral—behind-the-hand murmuring that he'd been hurt in Afghanistan. She hadn't even known he'd joined the Marines. She didn't know anything about him, really. Not since those dozen years ago when Daddy died and she and Mama left. Eli went the way of the pond—tucked into her memories, a piece of herself too precious to share.

"Wish I had binoculars," she mumbled, then shook her head at the nosey thought. She searched for a yellow dog trailing along the pond bank and someone sitting in the old fishing spot beneath the oak tree.

The oak tree.

A dull throbbing began in her chest as she traced the red pipe fence to a cross section T of barbed wire. The throbbing intensified.

There, in the farthest corner of her father's bottom land, stood an ancient oak, mutilated from some horrible incident, but alive.

How proud she'd been to show Eli. He was always the one discovering new things and marvelous sites, but she had found the great scarred tree on her own.

The dull throb sharpened to a pointed pain and she pressed a hand against her chest. From a distance the oak looked like the other hundred trees scattered over the hills, only bigger, strengthened by a horrific tragedy. A fire, Eli had declared with his irritating, know-it-all attitude.

"It's just a heartless old tree, Laura Bell, you ding-a-ling," he'd said. But she'd caught the wonder in his blue eyes.

"No, it isn't." She stomped her foot on the summer pasture. "It's a Miracle Tree. It has to be. How else could it be alive when there's no insides?"

They wiggled into the cavity and just fit—like two acorns in a squirrel's nest, their backs against the smooth shell. Lazy summer afternoons often found them there, guessing what had started the fire that ate away the tree's heart.

Blinking now didn't stop the tears, and they fell to fingers curled against the sharp pain.

Taking a shaky breath, she returned to the bedroom, opened her suitcase and found a pair of jeans and a T-shirt. She'd hike down to the tree first, then see about unpacking.

Eli Hawthorne never figured he'd prevent a city girl from doing a header in the roadside ditch, but the gal was right next to him when her skinny high heel snapped off and he couldn't just let her fall.

She mumbled a quick "thank you" without making eye contact.

Figured.

He made people uncomfortable.

After the little sports car shot up the hill, he mounted Buddy and rode down the slope toward the northwest section gate. He could do this with his eyes closed.

He snorted. What a laugh. With one eye gone, he was already halfway there.

He and Buddy ambled across the pasture, past the ranch house and into the barn where Eli unsaddled and brushed the gelding, then turned him out.

Goldie didn't hear the commotion and lay sleeping on her mat near the tack room door. Eli rubbed the old retriever's side and waited for her to get her bearings before he lifted her into the golf cart. She barked and fanned her thinning tail.

Loving eyes followed his every movement, and saliva dripped from her pink tongue. As a kid, Eli had thought she was smiling when she looked at him like that, her mouth pulled back in a grin. The gold had faded around her eyes and muzzle where white hairs outnumbered the yellow, and she needed his help getting in and out of the cart. No more bounding through the pastures while he fed the cattle.

He rubbed her ears and cupped her old head in his hands.

"Ready for a ride?"

She flicked her tongue and caught him on the nose—an old trick.

A distant screen-door slap jerked his gaze to the hill and memories popped to the surface like fishing bobbers. He squinted toward the house, but the front porch shadowed whoever stood there.

Laura Bell ran across his mind in her old sneakers and cutoffs, hair flying behind her like a horse's tail. He'd rarely climbed the hill when she lived there, because she'd always insisted the ranch was more fun than her house. Sometimes he'd meet her halfway up on a granite ledge where they'd sit and watch Goldie chase ground squirrels. He'd shoot at the chirping nuisances with his .22 and Laura would slug him and hide her face and cry when he hit one.

He chuckled to himself and scoped the hilltop, down the western side to the corrals and her dad's shop. When Mr. Bell died and Laura and her mother moved away, he'd tried to convince himself that life would be easier without that little pest tagging along behind him every minute.

But life hadn't gotten easier. Just emptier.

Goldie yapped impatiently and Eli climbed behind the wheel and glanced back at the hill.

Someone leaned over the deck railing and Eli froze.

From the porch, we can see everything, Laura had once told him. The slightest movement drew the eye, she'd said. He squinted again, trying to make out who it was. Man or woman, he couldn't tell.

The figure backed into shadow and Eli waited. In a moment, the person stepped off the porch and headed west, slowly descending toward the corrals.

Eli left the golf cart and walked in the opposite direction, across the yard on the east side of his house, keeping the hill in view. But the figure didn't go to the corrals and instead took the hairpin turn down an overgrown path that angled back toward the bottom land.

Eli stopped next to a tree, confident his dull clothing would blend in with the colorless bark. The reflexive action surprised him. Irritated him. This wasn't Afghanistan. He stood on his own property with every right in the world to be there. But he couldn't shake the training. He'd rather see than be seen.

The figure wore a ball cap but didn't walk like a man. Had to be that woman—new Realtor or new renter, though considering the sleek car she'd driven, he doubted she was a renter. He watched her saunter down, pause and look toward the house, then continue on. Where was she headed? The fence or the well?

At the bottom she picked up her pace and beat a straight line to the property's southeast corner. Each silent, distant step hammered in his chest. Only one other person knew about that corner and the importance of what stood there.

The hammering evened out to a steady throb and he half crouched, waiting for her to disappear behind the great oak. He assessed the distance to the next tree downhill, closer to his property line. When she stepped out of view, he made a run for it.

What a fool. Stalking a stranger on neighboring land. What if she saw him?

What if it was *her*?

"Don't be stupid," he muttered under his breath. That woman in the tight skirt was not Laura Bell.

A cold snout against his right hand jerked him around to see Goldie grinning and wagging her tail. How'd she get off the golf cart? Huffing a deep breath he reached for the old dog, but she edged away and limped off down the hill.

Toward the big oak tree.

Chapter 2

Laura inhaled deeply, filling her lungs and her soul with the pasture's warm earthy scent. Had it really been a dozen years since she'd walked this overgrown path? She stopped near the bottom and looked at her house poised like a ship on a high wave. Two granite ledges jutted out beneath the house, and ground squirrels taunted from the gray boulders. Stopping to scold her, they twitched their tails and chirped and then skittered between the crevices.

Memories tugged her lips into a smile and she turned toward the corner where her property line T-d against the Hawthorne Ranch's red pipe fence. Beyond the barbed wire on her left, the dirt showed through. The neighbor's scrawny cattle had grazed the spring grass down to nothing already.

To the south, Hawthorne land lay like a green blanket, protected from over grazing by good management. She wondered if Garcia still worked there, if Eli Hawthorne had come home after his tour of duty, or if there were new owners. Maybe that cowboy at the mailboxes.

She hoped not.

It was bad enough looking like a complete idiot in front of a stranger. She didn't need a neighborly reminder of what a klutz she could be.

As she neared the corner she picked up her pace, keeping her eye on the giant tree that anchored the pasture. Tears threatened at the sight of its tragic beauty, and she was a child again, running to crawl inside its big hollow heart.

Thick bark lipped over the edges of a deep scar, and the tree stood as if supported by only the outer skin. No core, no solid trunk like other trees, just a stiff, crusty mantel that held it upright.

She still didn't understand how something could survive such damage and live wrapped around an empty space where once a heart had been.

But she knew what it felt like.

Leaning in, Laura pressed her hands and face and body against the rough, ridged skin and closed her eyes.

"You live," she whispered, and tears squeezed out beneath her lashes. "Teach me how you live without a heart."

A nudge at the back of her knee sent her whirling to face a smiling dog, its ragged tail sweeping the air.

After a deep, steadying breath, she stretched a cautious hand toward the animal and it licked her fingers.

"Goldie?"

A whine rolled from the dog's throat and it stepped in closer, pushing its head against her leg. Laura dropped to her knees and searched the retriever's cloudy eyes. "Is it really you after all this time?"

The dozen years hadn't been kind to Goldie, either.

Laura swiped at her tears and sank back against the tree. The dog stretched out, its head in her lap. How had Goldie known she was there?

She scanned the Hawthorne pastures. Smaller oak trees scattered over the low hills, and an occasional black cow and calf, but no people. No Eli or Garcia.

She'd love to see them again, sit at the big kitchen table drinking cold root beer, listen to Garcia call Eli *muchacho tan feo*—ugly little boy. How sweet to sail again in the tire swing at the barn, follow Eli down to the pond…

Goldie let out a long sigh.

"Who do you live with, ol' girl?" She stroked the dull, yellow hair. "Did you ever have puppies?"

"A couple of litters."

Laura's hand and breath both stopped and she stared at the dog.

"Had the first pups a year after you left."

The voice came from behind her, near the pipe fence. Afraid of what she'd see, she peeked over her shoulder.

A cowboy stood on the other side, one boot planted on the bottom pipe, his arms draped across the top. A lopsided grin she'd recognize anywhere slid to one side, weighted down with a black eye patch.

It couldn't be.

Goldie hefted herself to a sitting position and yipped a welcome as Laura dug deep for her voice.

"Eli?"

He climbed up, swung a leg over and paused. "May I?"

"Yes, of course." She stood, brushed off her jeans and fought the urge to run up the hill and hide under her car.

Eli Hawthorne III jumped to the ground, leaning to the right when he landed. An angular jaw, lean muscle and about six inches in height had taken over since she'd left him at the pond with his mouth open and his fishing line sagging.

He pulled his hat off, took a few steps forward and stuck out his hand.

"Welcome home, Laura Bell, you ding-a-ling." The grin cocked his mouth up on one side and knocked her back a full twelve years.

In spite of her discomfort she laughed and took his hand. A man's hand. Calloused. Warm. Capable of dislodging a resistant real-estate sign.

"I…I didn't recognize you earlier."

A familiar devilment sparked in his eye. "That was you?"

She felt the heat return and ducked her head, grateful for the ball cap's brim.

"May I join you?" he said.

Suddenly devoid of all her city refinement, she snugged her cap down.

"Sure." She gestured toward the tree. "Have a seat."

He leaned against the oak, left leg out straight, and set his cowboy hat upside down on the grass.

Laura took a spot near Goldie who grunted as she laid her head on outstretched paws and closed her eyes.

"How'd you know it was me?" she said.

"I didn't. Not until you asked about the puppies."

An uncomfortable idea slithered in. "You were spying on me?"

He laughed, a little too nervously, she thought.

"No, I—uh—I just followed her over." He nodded toward the sleeping dog.

Laura plucked at a dandelion. "How do you suppose she knew I was here?"

Eli's mouth twitched but he didn't say a word.

"I think she understands English." Laura steepled her knees and linked her fingers around them.

"And Spanish," he said.

She cocked her head with a quiet laugh, remembering. "You're right. Sometimes she'd run the other way when Garcia scolded her." She looked at Eli. "Is he still around?"

"Yes and no." Eli's one eye held her gaze for a long moment, then shifted. Clear blue-gray like she remembered. Like the pond.

"He's still here, but he's gone this week. His granddaughter's getting married Saturday in San Diego. He'll be back Sunday."

"I don't remember her."

"She was never around. Lived with her parents down south."

He tugged at a grassy tuft. "She spent a few weekends here after you left, but never really took to the country. Didn't like to fish."

Laura warmed beneath his teasing glance and relaxed a little. "Would you believe I never went fishing again after we moved?"

"No. I wouldn't believe it."

She leaned back on her hands and lifted her face to the sun. Derek would have had a fit if she'd suggested such a thing.

Goldie whimpered and her eyelids fluttered.

"Chasing rabbits?" Laura said.

"Nope. Geese."

"How do you know?"

"She told me."

"You're still full of stories, aren't you, even after all these years."

He looked stricken. "But they're all true."

"Yeah. Like the one about a giant blue-bellied trout that lived in the pond. There's no such thing as a blue-bellied trout."

One side of his mouth slid up. "But you didn't know that."

"Not when I was ten." She looped her arms around her knees and rested her chin on top. "I believed everything you said back then."

His brows hitched together in a quick frown and he adjusted the patch. "Sorry to hear about your mom."

"Thanks."

Fighting tears at his sudden change of topic, she focused her attention on the scrubby growth shadowing his chin, and the hatband dent that creased his straight brown hair and marked a forehead two shades lighter than his face. He shot a look her way and she marveled to see the boy in the man.

He jerked his head toward her hilltop. "You come back to sell the place?"

"No."

Surprise quirked his left eyebrow. "So that's *your* silver bullet?"

She smiled, sat up straighter.

"Where'd you learn to drive?" he asked. "The Autobahn?"

"Funny." She wrinkled her nose at him.

"Seriously. When I heard it coming, I thought it'd been shot out of a gun. Did you forget about the S-curve?"

She raised her chin and looked down her nose. "No, I didn't forget about the S-curve. That car can handle it. So can I."

He snorted. The same snort that used to make her so mad she could kick him.

"I see you haven't changed," she said.

Her remark drew a dead-level, one-eyed stare.

"I mean…"

"I know what you mean." He ripped out a handful of grass and tore it into tiny pieces. "It's almost good to hear, considering."

"What happened?"

He tugged at the patch. "Shrapnel. They tried, but couldn't save it. Just as well, because it hurt like…" He shot her a quick glance. "Crazy."

Her heart squeezed. "It must be hard—riding and all."

"You adjust. Compensate. Make concessions." He tossed the grass in the air along with a question. "So you looking for a renter?"

She studied the house atop the hill. "No. I *am* the renter."

He didn't make a sound but she felt a snap in the air, like an unseen electrical current. She was afraid to look at him.

A sudden squawk jolted her upright and she turned to see a large Canada goose ogling them from the other side of the pipe fence. It honked again and aimed a black button eye as if sizing them up for the kill.

Eli picked up a pebble and side-armed it at the bird. It hollered again, flapped its great wings and waddled away. He popped off another small stone and the gander flounced up the hill, angling toward the pond.

"Pest," he said.

"Friend of yours?" She couldn't hide the amusement spreading across her face and rippling through her body.

"He thinks." Eli snorted and shook his head. "He thinks he's a dog. *My* dog."

She fell back in the grass and laughed until tears seeped from the corners of her eyes. She hadn't laughed in a long time and it felt good.

"It's really not that funny," he said, and flicked a pebble at her tennis shoes.

Struggling to catch her breath, she pushed up on her elbows. "It is to me."

He conceded a half smile. "You're really something, Laura Bell, you—"

"Don't you dare call me that." She jerked off her cap and threw it at him, and her hair uncoiled and fell over her shoulder.

His one-handed grab caught the missile and he stared.

"What?"

"You… Nothing." He tossed back the cap.

She twisted the strands together and tucked them under her hat, all the while watching him push to his feet.

He reached for his cowboy hat and offered to help her up. "It's good to see you again. I never thought you'd come back."

She took his hand and its warmth seeped into her skin. She remembered Derek's cold thin fingers and shoved both hands in her jeans pockets.

"I thought I'd give it a year, get a job substituting this fall in Spring Valley."

"I figured you'd be married by now with a couple of kids."

She looked past him to the oak tree, studied the scar for a long moment. "Almost."

He followed her gaze and ran a hand down the curved lip of the long wound. "Sorry. It's none of my business."

She shrugged, took a deep breath and pushed it out between tight lips. "It's okay. We've all got wounds. Some just show more than others."

She moved closer to the tree, splayed her fingers on the bark and leaned against her hands. "I'm so glad it hasn't changed. When we first moved away I was afraid it would fall over or be hit by lightning and burn."

Eli reached higher up the trunk. "These old oaks are pretty hardy in a grass fire. And it's been a while since we had one burn through the valley."

"I'm glad it's still here."

"Remember how we used to fit inside?" A true smile lit his face.

"Like two acorns in a squirrel's nest."

He chuckled. "That's what Pop said."

"How is he?"

"Gone." Eli didn't move or change expression or offer an explanation.

"Well." She took a step back. "Maybe I'll see you around."

His gaze locked on her again and she felt scrutinized.

"Yeah," he said.

He leaned over and patted Goldie on the side. "Come on, girl. Time to go home."

The dog raised her head as if testing his intent, then sat up with a grunt.

"I was so surprised to see her." Laura bent to hug the yellow neck. "I'm amazed she's still alive. How old is she now?"

Eli squatted, cupped Goldie's muzzle in his hand and looked her in the eye. "Nearly fourteen. She won't be around much longer."

Close enough to smell the dust and sweat on his clothes, Laura also heard the catch in his voice and her throat tightened. "You didn't keep any puppies?"

"Wish I had." He stood and adjusted the patch, tugged on his hat brim. "Come over sometime. We'll go riding."

"To Slick Rock?"

He jerked his head down in a single nod. "Yeah. To Slick Rock."

Chapter 3

The next morning Eli dumped soft-chew food in Goldie's barn dish, climbed onto the four-wheeler and drove to the west side to move sprinklers. One at a time he hooked them to the quad and pulled them through access gates into neighboring pastures, then set them to run for a couple of hours. He'd move them again around noon.

Subtle but certain, the emerald hills around his valley acreage were fading, and without water the pastures would dry up, as well. Then he'd have to buy more hay and his cow-calf pairs would eat him out of business.

Water meant life.

Moving sprinklers took longer without Garcia's help, but Eli needed the exertion. Something to block the recurring vision of Laura's hair tumbling down in a black wave. His heart kicked in time with the pulsing water arcing over the fence lines. When he saw her at the tree yesterday in jeans and a ball cap, she looked more like what he would expect—not the slick city gal from the sports car earlier. He wondered—which was the real Laura?

Satisfied with the sprinklers, he took the dirt lane to the bottom pasture and Lady H.

The mare grazed unhurriedly, her bronze coat a bold contrast to the pasture's deep green. A week-old filly walked close by, all leg with a bottlebrush tail and enough spunk to toss her head and prance a few steps away. But not far. Not yet. She trotted back to nuzzle her mother's flank and to tell the world with a twitching tail that life was good.

Eli once believed that himself.

He turned his head to see the pair more fully. Pop would have been pleased—though not with the bottom line. Developers feeding off the bad economy had already offered to buy the place. Eli couldn't bear to see it converted to a country club and golf course. Though he may have to put a few links out on the southeast end himself if any more calves disappeared.

He gripped the handlebars tighter at the thought of someone steeling his profits and turned toward the barn. Weeds crowded the drainage ditch. Pop would never have let things get out of hand or overgrown. When he ran it, the ranch looked more like a Kentucky horse farm than a small cattle operation.

After Afghanistan, eighteen months of rehab convinced Eli that he could return to the ranch, that he could carry his end of the load. But finding Pop slumped against the tractor one morning nearly did him in. Garcia helped get Pop into the truck and to the hospital, but they both knew it was too late. Elijah Hawthorne's heart had failed him.

Eli parked in the barn's shade and turned off the engine. He looked out over the pastures, the oaks, the black mamas and their babies, and the truth stirred deep in his gut. Pop's heart hadn't failed him at all. It had taken him out one more time and let him die doing what he loved, not cinched down in a hospital bed.

Eli hoped he'd do as well when his time came.

A cold wind rushed through his heart and in his memory he launched again from the Humvee, landing hard against a wall.

Death knelt beside him, watched his life pool dark and thick in the dust. Numb and deaf, Eli closed his eyes and saw the cattle, the pond and Laura. His prayers had gone unanswered.

A medic stopped the bleeding.

Later, Eli wished he hadn't.

Goldie whimpered and the ranch came into focus. Eli rubbed both hands over his face, trying to scrub the recurring vision from his mind.

He stepped off the quad and filled the dog's water dish and left her to sleep.

Maybe his prayers *had* been answered. This ranch was home and he loved it, regardless of where he'd been and what he'd done and what had happened to him. And it was Garcia's home, and Goldie's.

The irony cut deep. His family consisted of an old cowboy and a crippled dog.

He took his hat off and slapped the dust from his jeans as he headed for the house. In spite of the poor livestock market and high fuel cost, and in spite of the loss of his eye and foot, one good thing had finally happened. The one thing he'd dreamed of on long cold nights in the treeless mountains of a distant land.

Laura Bell had come home.

The first bed Laura had shopped for she hadn't actually shopped for. She'd merely trailed Derek through an outrageously expensive furniture store. At the time, it didn't matter what he chose. She was too enamored by her handsome, investment-banker fiancé, and if he had chosen a cot she would have agreed. But for him, appearances were everything, and men delivered a monstrous bed to the condominium the next day, with matching armoire, nightstands and a massive dresser.

It took her only a week to loathe it.

Seated on the front porch swing in cutoffs, she crossed her legs beneath her laptop and scrolled through a forest of Pinterest search results for brass beds. Hundreds of pictures popped up: ornate with frilly spreads and matching curtains, starkly plain with minimalist linen. Single, double, queen, king. Knobbed, railed, polished and aged. But she recognized it when she saw it—simple, sleek, with matching finials atop each of the four posts. A modest quilt and thick pillows softened its strong lines. She clicked on "double" and placed her order through the source site. She'd find a quilt in town.

Closing her computer, she gazed down at the Hawthorne Ranch. The sprinklers vaulted over the paddocks, and cow-calf pairs grazed in the upper pastures. A red-tailed hawk soared across her view and drew her eyes with its effortless climb. As a child she'd watched the regal birds for hours, knew where they nested, learned how they rode the thermals.

Why couldn't she glide through life like that?

Frustrated, she went inside and an answer trailed her to the shower. *You're not rising on the heat.*

Heat she understood.

The burning shame and anger of finding Derek with another woman the week before their wedding.

The scorching loss of her mother to cancer at the age of forty-seven.

Yes, she understood heat. She just hadn't figured out how to rise on it.

What did that even mean?

After her shower she stood dripping in the tub with the sudden realization that her overnight bag held all the essentials except a towel. She finger-squeegeed her arms and legs and finished with a clean T-shirt. As she dressed, she mentally ticked off a shopping list. Towels. Bathroom rugs. Dishes, pots and pans—she needed so much.

When she left Derek, she'd left everything connected to him. The ring, the dress, wedding gifts, shower gifts, everything they had picked out together. Except the roadster. *She'd* picked that out.

And when her mother died, she left everything else in the bungalow they had rented, other than her clothes and Daddy's shotgun. Not much else would fit in her car.

How could her life have fallen apart all at once?

Refusing to sob through another day, she combed out her hair, scribbled her list and locked the door.

On the way into town she let the wind toss her hair. She parked on Main Street and twisted the damp strands in a scrunchie. Determined to buy as much as she could afford from small business owners, she entered a narrow storefront offering "Linen, Luxuries and Life's Essentials."

The proverbial bell above the door announced her entrance, and the spicy atmosphere promised possibilities. A slender middle-aged woman approached from the back. She wiped the corners of her mouth with a paper napkin, then tucked it in the pocket of her long broom-handle skirt.

"Sorry about that." She thumbed her mouth self-consciously. "My granddaughter baked snicker doodle bread for me this morning, and I can't stop eating it." She held out her hand. "I'm Mary Travers."

Laura did a quick once-over thinking the name sounded familiar.

The woman noticed.

"Like Mary Travers of *Peter, Paul and Mary* fame," she said.

Laura nodded, still uncertain.

"You're much too young to know who they were, but your grandparents might have." She smiled. "I sing like a squeaky rocking chair, so I claim no connection to the folk group. Just my luck to marry a man with the name Travers."

Laura returned her smile. "I'm Laura Bell."

Mary fingered a faded brown strand behind her ear. "How can I help you?"

Laura pivoted and took in her surroundings: a clutch of bright copper kettles, specialty tea boxes and herbs, a wine rack stuffed with skeins of yarn. She could spend a fortune— a fortune she didn't have.

"The sign said Linen. Do you have quilts and bedding? I just moved here and I need a few things."

"Oh—newly married?" Mary turned toward a back corner and revealed a long braid that hung nearly to her waist. She wove through displays and stopped before tall wicker shelves bulging with sheets, blankets, tablecloths and towels.

"No. Suddenly single."

Mary sighed. "I'm sorry."

"Don't apologize, please. Starting over is still starting over. No one throws you a cancelled-wedding party."

Mary cringed. "I always pry when I shouldn't."

Laura squeezed a plush terrycloth towel. Pricey, but maybe she'd splurge.

"Are your quilts handmade?"

"Yes, but they're not antique." Mary lifted the lid on a wicker trunk and pulled out several folded quilts in various patterns and colors. "What size are you looking for?"

Laura spotted a simple multi-colored design and pulled it from the stack. "Double, if you have it. How big is this one?"

Together they stretched it out in the cramped corner.

"Looks like this should work," Mary said. "If you want to try it and it doesn't fit, you can always exchange it for something else."

Laura shook her head. "That's what I love about small-town merchants. Personal service and unheard-of concessions. You just sold a quilt."

As well as new bedding, towels, matching throw rugs, a designer shower curtain and kitchen linen; a hand-thrown pottery set with place settings for four and matching mugs also caught Laura's eye. Pots and pans would have to wait for the next trip, but she was certain she could fit the cute wicker animal bed with a red cushion on the passenger-side floorboard. And a handblown, glass orb hummingbird feeder.

Lighter in heart and bank account, Laura pulled through a fast-food place for chicken strips and then stopped at a hardware store for mouse traps, poison and a broom. She'd have to come back for a toolbox, hammer, screwdrivers and other essentials, but first she'd look in the shed at the corrals. Her mother may have left some of her dad's things behind—if they hadn't been taken by renters over the years.

The convertible drive was decidedly cooler once she left town and started the slow climb into the foothills. Before long, summer would wick the moisture from the hills and they'd fade to a tawny gold. She'd missed the spring wildflowers— purple and yellow and white—and blankets of copper poppies. But she could still plant annuals in the beds around the house.

More shopping. She smiled.

Turning left onto the county road, she geared up on the long straightaway, but changed her mind and slowed as she approached the ranch entrance. A long wooden sign with an oak tree silhouette hung above the gate, and deep-cut Western letters announced Hawthorne Ranch. Beyond it a rider circled in the round pen. Only the top of his hat showed over the high railing.

She returned her attention to the road, threaded the S-curve like the eye of a needle and stopped at the mail boxes to find hers empty. Disappointment pushed against her earlier good mood. Nearly all her communication she handled online. Efficient and impersonal. But for some odd reason she longed for a letter, handwritten words on real stationery, folded and sealed in a hand-addressed envelope. Something that said she was worth the extra time and effort.

She'd seen her mother's old love letters from Daddy. They seemed so much more personal than email and texts and instant messages.

But people didn't write letters anymore.

And besides, who would write her?

Chapter 4

The colt jerked its head up and shied away from the fence. Nearly unseated, Eli reined it in, berating himself for letting his mind wander. The culprit waddled past the rails.

"Little far from the pond, aren't you?"

The goose peered through the railing and honked, sending the colt hopping on all fours again.

"Easy—easy." Eli hushed his voice and pulled lightly, a steady hand on each rein, guiding the horse across the round pen to the other side. If Goldie wasn't sleeping in the barn, that gander wouldn't be squawking up a storm. That was all he needed—to get thrown with no one around to help. Garcia wouldn't be back until Sunday, and Eli would never hear the end of it if the aging *vaquero* returned to find him busted up.

He tugged at his eye patch, grateful the colt hadn't tossed him. Blind on one side, he might have missed a high-flying hoof. Garcia was right—he needed to work smarter, not harder. And a one-eyed cowboy with a missing foot on a green-broke colt with no one around wasn't exactly smart.

He circled the colt again, dismounted and led it through the gate. After unsaddling and a good rubdown, he turned the colt out in a small paddock where it bolted away, twisting and kicking its back legs like a yearling rather than a three-year-old.

As he watched, a glint of sunlight on glass caught his eye. Laura's bullet car poised on her hill's western slope again. He hadn't heard her return.

He pulled his hat off, rubbed his sleeve across his brow and headed for the golf cart. He loaded Goldie in the back, grabbed his tackle and took the lane over the irrigation canal, along the apple orchard and around to the pond. He parked under the oak and Goldie stood, wagging her tail and barking. Cradling her in both arms, he set her on the ground, and she limped along the water's edge yapping at the indulgent mallards.

Content in his old haunt, Eli baited a hook, plunked in the line and leaned back in the cool grass. Not so long ago Goldie would have been *in* the water with those ducks. He snorted. Time had done a number on them both. They'd never be what they once were, and they'd both learned to compensate.

He hated that word and everything it stood for, but it ruled his life. Compensation had become second nature when he lost his eye. And he compensated for his left leg, though a prosthesis kept him on both feet. One foot, technically. He could ride, had learned to balance himself by watching his boot in the stirrup. The same way he'd learned to walk again, by watching the ground where he stepped. But nothing could substitute for the eye and peripheral vision on the right side. An artificial orb gave him a normal appearance to other people, but not to himself, and that bothered him. He preferred the patch, though most of the time he felt as if he was about to be blindsided. Like he'd been blindsided in Afghanistan.

His pole dipped and he worked the line. A snag or a smart fish, for he reeled in a shiny hook with nothing on the end. Laura would have laughed.

Surprised at the trail his thought had taken, his gaze settled on the long gray house. He'd been truly sorry to hear about her mom. Lauraine Bell was a good woman, even though Eli had long resented her for moving away.

The day Laura had run to the pond with tears striping her flushed cheeks, she'd sobbed out the news. Her father was dead and they were leaving.

At fourteen, gangly and pimpled, Eli hadn't had the guts to tell a twelve-year-old that he didn't want her to go.

An old hunger clawed in his stomach. For years he'd carried the unlikely hope that Laura would return so he'd never gotten to know the renters who moved in and out and in. Later, he'd wanted to buy the place, and knew Ken Pennington did, too, the rancher east of Laura's twenty acres. But until Eli figured out who was stealing his calves, he wouldn't be buying anything.

Anger bubbled to the surface and his fists clenched. God help the man or men he found rustling his livestock.

He gathered his tackle and called Goldie to the cart. He needed to forget about the Bell place, at least for a year. If Laura settled in and stayed, she wouldn't be selling anyway.

And he'd rather have her as a neighbor again than have her land.

Laura stashed her new purchases and walked through the house, looking in closets and checking window latches. It felt so empty without furniture, but she'd already spent a bundle on the bed, linens and dishes, and she needed a vacuum cleaner. She closed the vents in the other two bedrooms at the opposite end of the house, shut the doors and turned on the air-conditioning. No sense cooling rooms she didn't use.

Grabbing the leftover chicken from the counter, she opened the refrigerator and gagged. She didn't even have baking soda. Realizing again how much she needed, she plopped down on the sofa with the last cold chicken strip to make another list. The bed should be delivered within the week and—

A knock at the French doors startled her. She hadn't heard a car drive up.

A man stood with his back to the doors. He turned at the click of the knob and she recognized an older version of her neighbor to the east—Ken Pennington. No wonder the hillside beyond her fence was so barren. He still lived there.

Pennington took off his hat and nodded.

"I live on top there." He jerked his head toward the road that continued back into the hills. "I was out riding and noticed your car. Are you interested in buying this place?"

She looked beyond him to the saddled buckskin nipping at the remains of her dead lawn. Pennington followed her gaze.

"Oh, don't mind him. The grass has been dead here for about a year, ever since the last renter moved out." He fingered the brim of his dirty felt hat. "But I keep an eye on the place for the property manager, now that the owner's passed on and all."

"Really."

"Yes, ma'am." He held out a meaty hand. "Name's Pennington."

Her fingers tightened on the doorknob. "I'm Laura Bell."

An open-handed slap would have drawn the same reaction, and he stepped back. His eyes raked her from top to bottom before he closed his mouth and cleared his throat. "I didn't recognize you, Laura." He fumbled with his hat. "You're all grown up. And mighty pretty, too."

"Thanks for stopping by." She started to close the door and he stuck a boot over the threshold.

A greasy smile stretched his lips. "Will you be staying? I mean, isn't this place for sale? I was thinking about buying the land myself, you know. Make you a good offer."

She stared at his boot until he pulled his foot back.

"No, thank you. It's no longer on the market. Goodbye, Mr. Pennington."

She closed the door and turned the lock while he stood on the porch running a hand around the inside of his hatband. She retreated to the living room where she could still watch him without being seen. After a long moment he lumbered down the porch steps, untied his horse and hefted himself into the saddle. She pitied the horse.

As he turned the buckskin toward her driveway, she moved to the kitchen window over the sink and watched them amble down her drive and out to the lane. He headed up the hill that folded into several more rising a couple hundred feet above her to the east. She shivered.

Her mother hadn't liked Pennington and neither did she. God forgive her for being rude, but her instincts told her not to trust him. A childhood memory drew her eyes to the kitchen corner where the barrel of Daddy's shotgun had rubbed a gray spot on the wall. She'd forgotten a lot about country life over the years, but she hadn't forgotten how to shoot.

Mama insisted the gun was for snakes. The "two-legged kind."

She understood now better than she ever had and was glad she'd held on to the old gun. Returning to the sofa she added to her list. Shotgun shells.

Saturday morning a van stopped in front of the house and the driver unloaded a large, flat box. Laura signed for the delivery, locked the door and watched him drive away.

One of her shiny new kitchen knives slit the box's taped edges, and she dragged out the padded bulk of a brass footboard. The headboard came next, followed by the frame, cross supports and a bag of screws.

Her newly adopted black-and-white kittens chased each other in and out of the empty box, and wrestled with the Bubble Wrap.

Within an hour, the bed stood against the outside wall of her bedroom. Its smooth patina gleamed like a family heirloom—minus a mattress and box spring.

"Where is my brain?"

She dropped to the floor in defeat and Pete and Re-Pete galloped from the living room through the bedroom door and into her lap. Their rolling ball-of-fur antics dashed her frustration and soon she was laughing at their clownish commotion. Of all the other animal shelter offerings, they had been the most aggressive, and she expected them to become good mousers. Their entertainment value proved to be a bonus.

In the kitchen she thumbed through an old phone book for a furniture store she'd seen in town. Hopefully, they had mattresses and would deliver. Otherwise she'd have to resort to the internet again.

After talking to a helpful employee who assured her the double mattress and box spring would be delivered by early afternoon, she flipped through the yellow pages under "Churches" and found the number for Spring Valley Chapel. A recorded message provided the service time—Sunday morning at ten-thirty. No evening or midweek services.

Pete and Re-Pete bounded into the kitchen and paddled across the slick floor like cartoon characters.

"Do you think I should invite Eli to go to church with me?"

The littermates arched their backs and sashayed around each other, then slammed together in mock battle.

"I'll take that as a no."

The troops followed her to the laundry room where she stuffed her new sheets into the washer.

"He wasn't wearing a ring the other day," she told Pete. Or was that one Re-Pete? "So I don't think there's a *Mrs.* Eli Hawthorne." Not that a missing ring meant anything. She added detergent and turned the setting to hot water. "But cowboys don't always wear rings, you know."

The kittens launched against her feet.

"In their line of work, a ring could cost them a finger."

Or a heart.

She thumbed the fourth finger on her left hand and dropped the lid on the washer.

At least the appliances worked.

She shut the kittens in the laundry room with a scoop of cat food and fresh water, filled a glass with ice and ginger ale, grabbed her laptop and went outside to settle on the front porch swing. She'd not planned ahead very well, and her needs didn't come to mind until they came into view—or failed to. Like a small table next to the swing. She set her glass on the porch floorboards and opened her laptop to check her e-mail. A whinny floated up from the ranch and she looked down on the neat rectangular sections, dirt lanes and white ranch house that had been in Eli's family for generations.

Would he go to church with her if she asked him?

When they were kids, Eli and his grandfather had attended most Sundays, slipping in the door after the singing was over. She'd annoyed her mother by repeatedly looking over her shoulder until Eli arrived. Then she'd thumb through the hymn book during the sermon and look for rhyming words to write on a paper tucked in her Bible.

The golf cart rolled into view and pulled her back to the present. A dog barked. It must be a ritual. Eli and Goldie were headed for the pond.

From deep inside an empty aching place, temptation rose to lead her running down the hill. Her memory squeezed between the fencing and raced to a small white rowboat banked at the pond. Closing her eyes, she dipped a bright blue paddle in the water while Eli leaned back and crossed his skinny legs on the center bench. He linked his hands behind his head, and a smug look of authority smeared his face. He always made her row. It was his boat, he said, and that was how she paid her way—by rowing. She sighed and opened her eyes in time to see him lift Goldie from the cart.

A heavy engine rumbled up the hill, and she hurried around front as the furniture store van made the tight turn into her driveway. The truck backed up to the yard, and two men carried in a plastic-wrapped mattress and box spring. She had them place the box spring in the frame and lean the mattress against the wall. Two minutes later they headed back down the hill.

She pulled off the plastic, spread a crisp red dust ruffle across the box spring and dropped the mattress in place. As she opened the laundry room door, the kittens escaped in a furry blur and darted through the house and under the new ruffle. She transferred the sheets to the dryer and set the timer for thirty minutes.

In the meantime she'd start the snicker doodle bread recipe she'd found online. Ever since her costly trip to the boutique, her taste buds had been screaming for the unusual treat. She loved snicker doodle cookies, especially when they were chewy, just a bit underdone. Hopefully, her bread would taste as good as Mary's had smelled.

The recipe promised enough for two loaves. If it turned out well, she'd take one to Eli tomorrow afternoon. The invitation to church could wait. At least until she knew where he stood.

A lonely cry stabbed the night. Laura rolled over in the wash of moonlight and looked out on the surrounding hills. Within seconds Pete and Re-Pete leaped onto the bed and pushed beneath her pillows.

"You scaredy cats." She pulled their trembling bodies against her own and lay listening to the coyotes' eerie song. A long pause, and then a chorus of yips and yowls. The pack had made a kill. She shivered and hugged the kittens closer.

The loaded shotgun stood in the nearest corner, a silent ally if she needed it.

Remembering other full-moon nights, she slipped from the bed and into the living room. The pond lay like a silver shell in a vast dark sea, shimmering as if it glowed from within. An owl called nearby and the coyotes sang again.

"O Lord, it's all so beautiful. So strange yet familiar." She hugged her elbows and sighed. "How did I ever survive all those years in the city?"

Chapter 5

Spring Valley Chapel shriveled beneath an overgrowth of pines, eucalyptus and flowering shrubbery. Laura parked her roadster at the far end, away from any dripping trees. What happened to the groundskeeper?

The little A-frame church had once drawn brides from all over the state with its red stained-glass Rosetta above the altar and quaint knotty-pine interior. From the looks of its neglected condition, Laura doubted that any woman would choose it for a wedding site now.

The same ancient wooden pews offered familiar seating and she stepped into the fifth row back from the front, grateful for new cushions that softened the encounter. To her surprise, the small sanctuary filled quickly. A fair-haired man with kind eyes and a guitar led the congregation in contemporary worship songs that Laura knew. Following an opening prayer and the offering, the same man took his place behind the podium.

Laura fought an absurd compulsion to look over her shoulder for Eli and his granddad. She forced her thoughts from the childish habit and opened her Bible. What scripture had the pastor mentioned?

"Above all else, guard your heart."

The preacher looked right at her.

"For it is the wellspring of life."

She lowered her eyes and turned to Proverbs. Fine job she'd done protecting her heart.

The empty ache throbbed in her chest and she envisioned the old oak tree, scared and vacant. Hollow. The pain intensified, sharpened, burned through her chest and scorched her lungs. She pressed a hand against her ribs and struggled to catch her breath. *O Lord, help me. I don't want to make a scene.*

"Are you all right?" a woman near her whispered.

Laura smiled and nodded, willing her lie to mask the truth. The lady reached over and patted Laura's leg, then returned her attention to the front. Laura refused to look up. She knew the pastor was watching her, knew he saw the gaping hole where her heart should be. She had to get out.

During the closing prayer, she squeezed past the woman and her husband and hurried outside to a bathroom she remembered at the back of the building. Grateful to find it, she locked the door and leaned against the sink taking long slow breaths. How humiliating. This had never happened anywhere. What was going on?

Automobile engines came to life and she listened as people left the parking lot and turned onto the main road. She could outwait them, make her escape after everyone left. On second thought, someone might notice her car and come looking for her. She had to leave immediately.

Standing tall, she scrutinized herself in the narrow mirror. No mascara smudges. Other than a deathly pallor, she thought she looked okay. She splashed cold water on her cheeks, dried her hands on a paper towel and stepped outside.

A quiet peace hugged the chapel grounds and she walked around the front to find an empty parking lot. Maybe she'd pulled it off after all. As she passed the double front doors, one opened and the young pastor stepped out. She stopped abruptly, as if caught stealing the offering.

His easy smile revealed perfect teeth. "Good to have you visit us this morning." He offered his hand in greeting. "I'm Alex Berger, the pastor here."

She took his hand. "Hi. Laura Bell."

She clutched her Bible against her ribs and he glanced at her left hand.

"I used to attend here as a child." *He doesn't need to know that.*

"Well, I'm glad you returned."

With a polite nod she stepped away and continued toward her car.

"Come back."

She stopped.

"Next Sunday. Come back next Sunday. We'd love to have you again."

Embarrassment burned the back of her legs and arms, and she threw a forced smile over her shoulder. "Thank you." Sprinting would be rude, so she ordered her feet into a slow, methodical stride.

She backed out and eased past the chapel while Berger locked the front door. He turned with a cheerful wave, and she nosed onto the road and around a curve before shoving her foot on the gas pedal and shooting away.

On Sunday morning Eli glanced at the hilltop, connected the rolling sprinkler to the hitch on the quad and glanced again. The bullet waited next to the house. Why didn't she park in the carport at the other end?

He was late. Water should have been on the pasture before the sun evaporated nearly ten percent of it. He pulled the sprinkler into a neighboring pasture, unhitched and drove back for the next one. At the power surge, the sprayers coughed to life, building up pressure to send a gleaming arc over the thirsty ground. Within twenty seconds they pulsed at a steady rate, the heartbeat of the property.

Red-winged blackbirds trilled from cottonwood trees shading the ranch's central lane. The quad popped in and out of those long shadows as Eli returned to the barn. He switched to the golf cart, loaded a hay bale and drove to the feeder pen where a half dozen dairy calves crowded the fence. The ranch always bought bull calves from a dairyman friend, fed them out as steers and sold them later in the year. He hooked the bale and tossed it over. Sweet, dusty air swooshed up as he turned his head to the right and sneezed.

Still there.

At the south pasture where Lady H grazed with her foal he checked again.

No movement outside the house. The car waited.

He slipped between the pipes and talked his way to the mare, hoping her steady temperament would rub off on the baby. She snorted softly against the grass and swished her tail as he stroked her neck and withers. The filly angled away, wide-eyed and wary.

"Show her how you trust me, Lady." Laying his left arm over the mare's rump he walked around to her right side. Her ears rotated, one following him, the other tracking her foal. "It won't be long," he said in a soothing tone.

Lady lifted her head and whiffled her grassy breath against his chest, then returned to grazing.

He squeezed back through the fence, drove to the barn and found Goldie asleep on her pad. At the touch of his hand she opened cloudy eyes, struggling as if to remember. Then she pushed herself up and thumped her tail with a quiet woof.

He filled her dish with soft food, gave her fresh water and headed to the house for his tackle.

A quick glance confirmed it. Still there.

The back porch screen door popped behind him and a sudden caffeine craving drove him to the kitchen. Garcia would be back sometime today. None too soon. He could use the company.

"Since when do I need company?" he asked the window over the sink that framed a perfect view of Laura's hill. The car hadn't moved.

What was it about Laura Bell that drew his curiosity to the hilltop? Longing crawled into his gut, a boy's unanswered prayers stuck on replay. He snorted. "Finally she's back and here I am, half a man."

The irony of his self-inflicted judgment soured in his stomach. He started the coffee and sat down at the kitchen table.

Running his hand across the plastic cloth, he recalled the old blue checkered fabric his grandfather had used until it fell apart. He easily envisioned a scrawny girl in the other kitchen chair, honey-brown legs dangling above the floor, eyes the color of cold root beer.

The coffeepot hissed out a final drop and his stomach knotted.

He filled a travel mug, gathered his tackle box and pole from a long wooden table on the back porch and strode down the steps, across the lawn and into the dirt lane toward the barn. He refused to look back.

He would not look back.

He looked back.

Over the top of the house and right of the massive cottonwood, he could see the empty spot. The car was gone.

He stopped.

His heart double-clutched and he checked his watch. Time for church.

The pole balanced in his fingers as he waited. Any minute the silver car would shoot out between the two granite boulders at the bottom of the S-curve and jet into the long stretch past the ranch.

As he watched, an old red pickup rattled by. Travers, a neighbor farther up the road. Eli's fists clenched around the pole and his mug. Had he missed her? Did she slip by while the coffee perked? No. He would have heard her shifting gears for the straightaway.

A meadow lark called from the pasture behind the ranch house, and the car eased through the gap more slowly than he'd expected. It cruised past the ranch, out of sight, and geared down for the T at the end. The engine faded to the west. Toward the chapel.

He hadn't been back since Afghanistan.

At the barn he found Goldie resting on her pad, her food half-eaten.

"Come on girl. Time to taunt the geese and catch a fish." Her eyes blinked open and followed him as he set his gear on the front seat.

"Yeah, I know. Good thing I'm such a great fisherman." He bent to lift her to the cart's back deck where she sat and barked. He powered out of the barn and took the familiar lane over the ditch, past the orchard and out to the oak that shaded the pond. A familiar squawking floated over the water, and a fat black and brown goose scuttled toward the tree.

It wasn't the fishing he enjoyed so much as sitting by the pond with a purpose. Which was fishing. Eli baited the hook and tossed it in, thinking how Garcia would appreciate fried fish tonight when he got home.

Goldie shuffled along, yapping at the gander. The goose seemed to understand and waddled a step or two ahead, shaking its tail feathers and squawking just enough to keep the old dog in the game.

A tug on his line drew Eli back to his supposed mission and after a little coaxing he reeled in a good-size bass.

"Where have you been hiding all this time?" The large fish would feed both himself and Garcia. He hooked it on a stringer, dropped it over the bank, leaned back in the cool grass and closed his eyes.

A soft breeze played across his face and soon a subtle rocking lured him toward sleep. Laura rowed them across the pond and he peeked beneath heavy lids, watching her lean into the oars, a concentrated frown bunching her slender brows. She pulled the oars in and they drifted. For hours they drifted, in and out of light and dark, and he teased her and called her a ding-a-ling. How could he not with a name like Bell? She opened her mouth and whined, tight and high like a wrapped up engine…

He opened his eyes, sat up and rubbed his neck. A not-so-distant motor roared into earshot, dropped off, then steadily accelerated. He couldn't see the road from the pond, but he knew that engine. In about fifteen seconds, Laura would drop one gear as she hooked the bottom of the S. He hoped. The blind double curve at the top was bad enough, but combined with a heavy foot and a sports car, the curve could be deadly.

He held his breath and waited to hear the bullet shoot out the other side and climb the hill. Something had put lead in her foot today. The sermon? People she hadn't seen in a dozen years? From the way she took the climb it sounded as if she was either mad or running scared.

A latent defensiveness crept into his arms. A yearning to protect, defend. He scanned the hill behind Laura's place and locked on Ken Pennington's house wedged between striking gray granite monoliths. A glint of light sparked and disappeared. Field glasses?

Eli's pulse kicked up and the palms of his hands itched. With the right scope he could knock that spec out with a single shot.

He turned back to the pond and took a deep breath, concentrated on slowing his heartbeat. He couldn't go there, couldn't follow that thinking. He shook his head and tugged at the patch. An internal warning system flashed in the void that once held his right eye. What was the issue? Himself, or Ken Pennington?

Chapter 6

Laura's hand shook as she fumbled with the key. Pete and Re-Pete whined through the glass and she feared they'd dash outside.

"Get back!" She stomped her foot as she twisted the knob and they darted into the living room. Frantic, she turned the lock and leaned against the door, fear thudding in her chest. What was happening to her?

Be reasonable. Think this through.

Two black-and-white faces peeked around the corner.

"I'm sorry." She slid to the floor and held a hand out as the kittens warily made their way over. Satisfied that she wouldn't crush them, they threaded through her knees and purred their tiny welcome.

"God, what's wrong with me?"

She felt like the new kid at school, terrified of not fitting in, or being ridiculed. But she did fit in—this was her childhood home.

Except it wasn't.

She looked around the kitchen and through the archway into the living room. The house was structurally the same, but smaller. The rooms offered the same glorious valley view, but they were emptier. She had tried to regain what the twelve-year-old Laura had lost, and she realized she couldn't. She was choking through the trauma of separation and loss all over again.

Memories and reality were not the same thing, and she'd been foolish to think she could go back to how things were before she moved away. Before Mama died. Before Derek.

She stood and straightened her khaki skirt, smoothed her blouse and pushed her hair from her eyes.

Rise on the heat.

The strange directive soared above her thoughts.

"Lord, what does that mean?"

The kittens sat for a rare moment, staring at her, then trotted away to play with the dust ruffle.

The gnawing in her stomach interrupted her musings and demanded snicker doodle bread and milk. Pleased with the way the bread had turned out, she finished the remains of the first small loaf and wrapped the second in another layer of foil. Eli said Garcia would be back today. She could take it by as a welcome home gift.

Flimsy excuse.

She wanted to see Eli and the longing surprised her. Things weren't as they once were, and she needed to accept that fact. But still, a neighborly gesture wouldn't be so bad. Would it?

Would Eli take it the wrong way if she stopped by?

She changed her clothes and plopped into the porch swing, determined to get a handle on her emotions. The golf cart waited at the pond, the sprinklers spread their glittering arcs and the familiar pastoral scene settled her nerves.

"It *looks* the same, Lord, but I need You to give me fresh eyes. Help me not to dwell on what *was,* but on what *is.* Help me see the new before me."

She moved to the railing and leaned against the rough wood.

A metallic-green flash darted in and hovered at the hanging glass bulb. The tiny bird dipped a long thin beak into the ruby water, and zipped to the other side for a refill. A rival swept in and the two sparred and parried like miniature swashbucklers.

Unable to contain her laughter, Laura wondered where the hummingbirds nested. How did they know a new feeder hung from the porch after the house had stood empty for so long?

"Do you have internal radar?" she asked the duo.

Movement drew her eye to a white pickup easing down the central ranch lane. The golf cart motored out from under the oak by the pond, looped around the apple orchard and sped toward the tractor shed. The muted thud of a pickup door and Goldie's excited barking told her Garcia was home.

"So I see you did not break your neck in the round pen." Garcia's wide smile belied the sarcasm in his raspy voice.

Eli returned the man's grin and adjusted the patch. "Came close." He gripped Garcia's hand in their usual greeting and slapped him on the shoulder. "How was the wedding?"

Garcia shrugged and tipped his head. "Tamales, enchiladas." He patted a pouch above his belt. "What can I say? It was good, no?"

Eli laughed and held up the stringer. "No appetite for fried fish?"

"I did not say that." Garcia lifted a duffel bag from the truck bed and headed for a small house tucked into the trees. "I am an old man. A small *siesta* and I will be ready for your fried fish."

"Yeah, you're old and I'm the governor of California."

Garcia waved a hand in dismissal and Eli continued toward the main house. Goldie followed, temporarily rejuvenated by the excitement.

Garcia had been around for as long as Eli could remember. He'd stayed on through droughts and bad markets. Worked sometimes for nothing because there was nothing to pay.

Yes, he was old. And he was family.

Eli cleaned the fish outside under a free-standing spigot, took the fillets inside to bag in plastic and stuck them in the refrigerator. Then he scrubbed the smell from his hands. Goldie trotted through the kitchen and into the family room where she dropped onto a braided rug in front of the fireplace. A long sigh signaled an oncoming nap and Eli sat down at the desk to do paperwork.

The big rolltop desk was older than him, Garcia and Goldie all put together, and had been in the ranch house when his granddad bought the place. A wooden swivel chair with worn arms complained when he leaned back.

Eli pushed a hand through his hair and stared at the ledger book. He needed to do another head count. Last week two more calves vanished. He doubted that coyotes were to blame because they don't eat bones. A lion? Maybe. But he'd found absolutely nothing resembling a carcass. Those babies had simply disappeared.

Now that Garcia was back, they could split an all-night watch. It'd be hard working all day and half the night, but they had to figure out what—or who—was getting the calves, and Goldie was no more watchdog than that fish in the refrigerator. He looked at the old dog, paddling her feet again and thought of Laura and their so-called chance meeting at the oak.

If it hadn't been for Goldie, Eli wouldn't have had the courage to walk out there. He huffed out a snort. He had what it took to rush a nest of insurgents, but no guts at all when it came to Laura Bell.

The black eye patch hadn't repulsed her, but she didn't know the whole story yet. She might not be so friendly once she learned it.

A knock on the back door surprised him and he glanced at Goldie who kept right on dreaming. Garcia wouldn't knock.

He'd left the back door open, and on his way through the kitchen he saw her beyond the screen door. She stood in cutoffs, a tank top and tennis shoes, with something in her hand.

"Come in." Eli pushed the screen open as she stepped aside.

Laura held out a foil-wrapped loaf with a smile. "I tried a new bread recipe and thought you might like to try it, too."

"Perfect timing." He led her to the kitchen and set the bread on the counter. "I'm frying fish for a late lunch. Want to stay and see Garcia?"

Her shoulders relaxed. "Yes, I'd like that. If you have enough."

"I've got plenty. Caught a big bass this morning."

She stood near the stove, fingers tucked in her shallow pockets, taking in the kitchen. "Hasn't changed much."

"No need. Everything still works."

She moved to the table and ran a hand across the plastic cloth. "This is different." She looked at him. "Wasn't it blue checks?"

"Good memory." *And your eyes are still the color of cold root beer.* He tugged on his patch. "How 'bout something to drink?"

"Do you have root beer?"

Caught in his daydream, he felt warmth crawl up his neck. "Sorry, fresh out. Iced tea or water."

Her fluid laughter that spilled so readily in their childhood flowed across the space between them. She pulled out a chair. "With sugar, please."

He wanted to ask how things went at the chapel, but that would let her know he'd been watching her and predicting her movements. Not a good idea. He filled two glasses with ice, added sugar to hers and poured cold tea into both. Then he leaned against the counter and took a long sip.

"I went to the chapel today."

He choked on the first swallow.

Laura watched him—wide-eyed like the filly—waiting for him to catch his breath. "You all right?"

"Yeah—yeah, I'm fine." He sleeved his mouth and looked around for napkins. In the drawer. Right. He laid a couple on the table and took the other chair.

"I expected you and your granddad to walk in and sit in the

back row," she said. "Silly, I know, but it's an ingrained reaction. Last time I was there, you did."

She watched him over the rim of her glass as she took another drink, then set the glass on the table, both hands wrapped around it as if holding herself down.

"I haven't been there in quite a while." He cleared his throat. "Not since I got back."

A question arched her brows.

"From Afghanistan."

"When was that?"

Here we go. "Two years ago."

She didn't question him further, but took another drink and looked out the window above the sink. He knew from her low vantage point she'd see only the higher hills northeast of the ranch, and the branches of the cottonwood. Not her hilltop.

"It was hard," she said. "Going back, I mean. Too many memories." Her eyes shifted to his. "The preacher is nice enough, and he invited me back, but I don't know if I can."

Now it was his turn for a puzzled look and she read it.

"It's weird, you know? So much is the same and yet it isn't."

Goldie's nails clicked against the hardwood floor as she trotted into the kitchen. Laura's features softened when she saw the old dog, and she leaned over to hug its neck. Goldie rested her chin on Laura's bare knees and swept the air with her tail.

"I know what you mean," Eli said. "Like Goldie. She's the same but she isn't."

The screen door slapped.

"Mija." Garcia's scratchy voice pulled Laura from her chair, and she ran to throw her arms around his neck.

"Ah, mi Lorita, you are all grown up."

The man's black eyes twinkled with pleasure and he kissed Laura soundly on each cheek.

"It's so good to see you." She hugged him once more, then took another glass from the cupboard and filled it with iced tea. "I brought you something." Her gaze flickered to Eli and she added, "Both of you. I baked it last night."

Eli gave his chair to Garcia and brought one in from the dining room.

"So you have come to visit your *vaqueros?*"

Laura laughed. *"Si, abuelito."* Taking her seat, she leaned her arms on the table, across from the man she'd always called grandfather. "But I'm not here to visit. I'm here to stay."

Garcia drank long and hard, his eyes closed. Then he set the glass on the table and looked at Laura with a tenderness Eli suspected the man reserved for his recently married granddaughter.

"It is good." He nodded and a wide smile brightened his wrinkled face. "May you look down upon this *rancho* with the eyes of heaven."

Eli stared at the floor and darkness edged his vision. He doubted that heaven saw anything. It was the only point he and Garcia had ever argued over.

The silence stretched, as if the others waited for him to comment. He refused. Rising with his glass, he set it on the counter and dug out a large cast-iron skillet.

Chapter 7

Laura felt the tension snap between the two men. It surprised her, knowing the deep affection they held for each other. Something had happened to change one of them, not physically, but deeper. And she doubted that Garcia had changed.

While Eli dipped and breaded fillets, Garcia rubbed Goldie's side with his boot and talked about his granddaughter's wedding. Laura listened with an occasional smile as she sliced her small loaf, set the table and concocted a green salad with what she could find in the refrigerator.

Begging a silent blessing on the ancient buttermilk dressing, she tossed it into bits of wilted lettuce, soft tomato and dull bell pepper. Sweet bread, a pitiful salad and fried fish didn't exactly make a balanced meal, but it would have to do.

Another awkward moment hung over the table when Laura laid her hands in her lap and bowed her head. At the silence, she glanced up to see Garcia watching Eli and Eli cutting into his crisp fillet. As head of the house, Eli made no move toward prayer, so she picked up her fork and tried the salad. A quick peek at Garcia brought a sly wink from the older man's dark eyes and she bit the inside of her cheek to keep from giggling.

Goldie sat perfectly still next to Eli's chair, more alert than Laura had seen the dog so far. Somber eyes followed Eli's fork from plate to mouth and back again, but the jaw remained tightly clamped. No whimpering, begging, or drooling.

Eli cut the end from his fillet and pushed it to one side. His gaze slid to Goldie and his mouth hitched and threatened to smile.

"What brings you home, *mija?*" Garcia sliced a bite from his fish.

"Mama died and I decided not to sell the property." She sipped her tea and wiped her mouth on a napkin. "I'm going to give it a year, hopefully do some substitute teaching in Spring Valley."

The old man's dark eyes seemed to read all she hadn't said, and she felt tears pushing against her eyes. This wasn't the time or place, and she dropped her gaze to the hideous plastic tablecloth and tried to imagine who had picked it out.

"Home is *bien*. It is good to have you back." He nodded twice, picked up his glass and looked at Eli. "So, how many last week?"

How many what? Laura watched an unspoken conversation play across the men's features.

"Two."

Garcia winced, but just barely. Had she not spent years watching his dark, crinkled face, she wouldn't have caught it. His familiarity comforted her as much as the old scarred tree, but she sent up a silent prayer to see what was new. Her eyes drifted to his still-thick hair and she noticed the white at his temples. Elsewhere a few bright strands marked the deep black in striking contrast, unlike the fading brown she'd seen on Mary Travers.

Eli continued eating and didn't elaborate, so she inquired. "Two what?"

He slid a glance her way and the icy anger chilled her bare

skin. How could he change so quickly from warm and friendly to cold and distant?

"Calves. Two calves. That makes ten we've lost this year."

Still, she didn't understand. "Lost?"

"*Si.* It is not *coyótes*," Garcia intoned with the Spanish pronunciation. "Other than the two-legged kind."

Laura thought of snakes. "Someone's stealing your cattle?" Skeptical, her gaze passed from one man to the other. Cattle rustling went out with the Old West, she'd thought. Did people still do that in the technological age?

Eli tossed the saved fish portion to Goldie who caught it in midair. Garcia grinned and mumbled something in Spanish. Eli pushed his plate back and planted his forearms on the table.

"We've had a bright moon the past few nights so I think we're due for a late rise tonight. I want to post a watch." He addressed Garcia. "You up to half a night?"

Garcia nodded. "It will be hard to see them in the dark, but I will try."

Eli grinned, but it wasn't pleasant. "I've taken care of that."

Garcia's eyes glinted like polished onyx. "So, we will see them after all."

"Maybe I could help."

"No." Eli's sharp answer and the snap of his head set Laura back against her chair. He must have noticed, for his stony features softened as he considered her. "This is dangerous. Whoever's out there is taking a chance at getting shot. I don't want you in the cross fire."

A cold hand gripped her stomach. "Shot? You'd actually *shoot* someone?"

"No, *mija,* he will not shoot them. He will shoot *near* them. To let them know he sees."

Laura wasn't so sure. The look on Eli's face said otherwise.

He held her with his cold, blue gaze. "Do you have any idea what it costs me to lose a calf?"

She shook her head and stared back.

"Anywhere from four hundred to seven hundred a head,

depending on the market price. Multiply that by ten. I can't afford to lose any more."

"Can't you call the authorities?"

His lips curled into a snarl. "They already know. They're watching for my brand at the sale yards. But good thieves can run a brand—burn in a line or two to change it. Out of the county, and farther south across the border, people look the other way."

"This is true, *Lorita*. This is a hard time for many."

She swallowed and felt suddenly extravagant with her Mercedes, knowing what Derek had paid for it. In cash, no less. She straightened and raised her chin. "My offer still stands. You know where to find me." She scooted back and gathered the plates. "I'll wash, *abuelito,* if you dry."

"I'll get it." Eli stood and picked up the fish platter and salad bowl.

Laura refused to be pushed around by him, even if this was his house. She was his equal now, not a child. "You cooked. We'll clean."

She faced him squarely and silently dared him to argue. Regret flashed briefly in his expression, then he set down the dishes and strode out the back door.

She let out a heavy sigh as the screen smacked the doorframe.

"Is it really that bad, Garcia?"

"It is bad, *si.* But there is more."

Surprised by the older man's willingness to talk, she faced him and leaned against the sink. "What is it?"

Garcia scooted his chair back but remained seated. "He thinks he is a half man."

Horrified, she stared.

"When he returned from fighting, he returned without all of himself."

"You mean his eye? He thinks he's half a man because he lost an eye?" The Eli she'd grown up with would never have let that slow him down.

"No."

She hugged her waist and thought back to their first meeting. "I noticed he leans a little to the right."

"He has no left foot."

Garcia's stark explanation caught her in the chest, and her hand flew to her mouth. "I had no idea. I heard whispers at my mother's funeral that he'd been wounded, but I didn't know how badly." She turned to fill the sink with hot water and dish soap and hide her eyes.

"But he's whole, can't he see that? He's a whole man, strong and capable and...well, capable." She wanted to say *caring,* but his behavior at the table gave her pause.

"It is his heart that is cut in half, *mija.* Not his body."

At Garcia's words the throbbing returned to her chest. She shoved both hands into the hot soapy water, hoping the distraction would ease the pain.

Garcia brought the glasses and serving bowls to the sink. As Laura washed each dish, he took it from her, held it under running water and dried it with an ancient towel as thin and frayed as her emotions. When they finished, he laid a calloused hand on her shoulder.

"I see that you, too, have a wound, *Lorita.* You are missing something—like the boy from your childhood. Perhaps you can each fill up the other." He patted her lovingly. "But only God can heal *el corazon.* And our friend is not willing."

Laura watched Garcia walk out of the kitchen, across the back porch and into the slanting afternoon sunlight.

El corazon, he'd said. The heart.

With each throb of her aching chest, a new tear slid down her face and dropped into the tepid water.

Eli clenched the penlight between his teeth. A thermal imaging scope topped the Remington .223 slung across his back, and a pocket in his camo pants bulged with extra ammunition. Other pockets held a night vision monocular, water bottle and

Laura's leftover cookie bread, or whatever she called it. He shuddered at the thought of her out here in the dark.

He looked down, aimed the light and planted his left boot on the first of many slats that laddered up thirty feet to the barn's peak. Watching the boot, he pushed himself up. One. Two.

Darkness compounded the task. Three. He could have crawled up on top of his pickup. Four. Five. But he wanted the high ground, so to speak. Six, seven. And from what he'd seen on a trial run earlier in the day, the highest point other than Laura's front porch was his barn roof.

Ten. Eleven. Twelve.

He'd played up there as a kid, though Granddad would have skinned him if he'd known. Eli had nailed two-by-fours in a rough square around the skylight opening so he wouldn't roll off the slope. Fifteen. This was the one place he'd never taken Laura, though he doubted she would have balked at the risky climb and even riskier idea of a crow's nest perspective. Twenty-one. He knew she wasn't afraid, but he was. Twenty-four. Afraid she'd slip or get hurt somehow. After all, he was responsible for her. Or so he had thought.

Twenty-six.

The air grew dense and hot as he climbed, and on the twenty-eighth rung he stopped and aimed the light at the ceiling then back to the ladder. Two more steps and he bumped the skylight with his head. He killed the light, slid it into his shirt pocket and felt for the latch that would release the fiberglass pane.

Fresh air rushed across his face as he pushed the hinged panel back. It fell against the corrugated steel roof and he stopped cold. Stopped breathing. Waited for the click of a safety, the clink of metal on metal. The smell of sweat on a hidden man.

Nothing.

He tightened his grip and shook his head. Not Afghanistan. Accustomed to the barn's tomblike darkness, the starry brilliance surprised him. He filled his lungs with the sweet breath of nightfall on pastureland and pulled himself through the opening and into a sitting position. All around him quiet reigned.

A knob on his watch illuminated the face with a green *22:00*—10:00 p.m. Garcia would come on at two and watch until dawn. Not on the barn, but from a hill at the southern corner of the ranch. If all was quiet, Eli would sleep on the roof and climb down after daylight.

He closed the hatch and set out his water, monocular and ammunition. Cinnamon wafted up as he unwrapped the bread and bit into the sweet softness. He could get used to this— sweet Laura Bell and her sweet homemade bread.

He snorted in disgust.

Sweet chance of that after snapping her head off at dinner.

He crimped the foil around two remaining slices and laid it in the corner of his safety frame. Then he stretched out on his stomach, planted his elbows and raised the rifle scope to his eye.

Laura huddled on the porch swing. Wrapped in the quilt from her bed, she marveled at the starry blanket glittering above. No streetlights vied for attention. No neon, no artificial light at all. Even the Halogen at the ranch had been extinguished. Eli's doing, no doubt. She hugged her knees and scanned the ranch, wondering where he hid. With his military background, Eli would not be seen or heard.

She recalled his chilling gaze at the dinner table and pulled the quilt tighter.

Garcia said Eli considered himself half a man, but she saw it differently. More like two sides of the same man. Two completely opposite personalities. One side she recognized from their childhood—fun-loving, sure of himself. Quick to tease and lord it over her, yet watchful. Caring. The grown-up Eli had a sharp, defensive edge. He was guarded. Cold. Angry.

And if she'd heard Garcia right, Eli wanted nothing to do with God.

Crickets trilled from the pond, and a bullfrog bellowed in the rushes along the banks. From somewhere to her right an owl offered a throaty call, answered moments later by another. No coyotes whined, no dogs barked, no cars traveled the road that bordered the ranch. All the world slept.

Relaxing, she burrowed deeper into the quilt folds and the movement caused the swing to sway. She could sleep like this, cuddled beneath the stars, in the shelter of her porch.

And then a woman screamed.

Chapter 8

Laura's own cry strangled in her throat. She clamped a hand over her mouth and every fine hair on her arms stood erect. Staring into the dark hills above her house, she waited for the next outburst.

Again the scream sliced through the night and through her nerves, and her muscles flexed with the instinctive urge to run. She held her position, strained to see movement in the darkness and willed herself to breathe.

The chilling fear ebbed as reason flowed in on her father's dear voice. *She's far away, Laury, girl. Don't be afraid.*

The cry must have come from above Slick Rock, for it would have been louder had the cougar been anywhere close by. Laura thought of the lair above the falls that tumbled over the rock in the spring runoff. Beyond Pennington's land, a half mile east of her fence line. Close enough.

Her pulse hammered in her ears and pounded in her neck. She took long, slow breaths and scanned the ranch, listening for restlessness among the livestock. All lay still, as much as she could tell, and again she wished for binoculars. Better yet, night vision goggles like Eli and Garcia used. Could Eli see her from his lookout?

Slowly the crickets picked up their chorus, the bullfrog thrummed and the night whispered through the grass.

Rising from the swing, she gathered the quilt against her body and at the screen door stooped to peer through the bottom for the kittens. They tumbled in the kitchen, and she slipped in, softly closing the door behind her and turning the lock. Pete and Re-Pete bounded across the room and sank their claws in the dangling quilt corners. Chuckling, she dragged them to the bedroom and dropped them on the bed where they skittered to the floor and dashed beneath the dust ruffle.

Holding the quilt wide, she snapped it in the air and it floated to the bed in a silent flutter.

Just as the first shot rang out.

The riderless horse reared at the ping of steel on steel and a hunched figure scrambled through the pipe fencing and grabbed at the reins. One more kiss of steel on an upright post, and the horse spun and bolted up the draw behind the pasture, its rider in stumbling pursuit.

Eli smiled to himself, chambered another round and scoped the cattle bedded down nearby. Startled by the sudden noise, cows raised their hind quarters first and then stood facing the outer fence. Calves hugged close to their mothers' legs and bawled.

Eli trailed the fleeing man until he disappeared over the draw, his horse long gone ahead of him.

The thief wouldn't return tonight. He'd not turned his face toward Eli, so he wouldn't have seen the rifle's flash. He wouldn't know where the shot came from—only that he'd been found out. And from the way he moved, Eli doubted it was Pennington. A hired hand, maybe. Or someone else altogether. Who knew, these days?

He laid the rifle next to him, unwrapped Laura's bread, then rolled onto his back and gazed at the stars as he ate. Tomorrow he'd drive into town, have breakfast at the coffee shop and stop by the feed store. Chances were he'd hear some chatter. He wasn't the only rancher losing livestock in this economy.

Pin pricks needled Laura's abdomen and rhythmically pushed through her sleep shirt.

"Ow!" Bolting upright, she scattered the kittens kneading her stomach. She fell back against the pillow to get her bearings. Had she been dreaming? Leaning over the bed she reached under the dust ruffle and met with a teasing paw, claws sheathed.

"Come here, you rascals. What do you think I am—your mother?" She could hear their tiny motors running and scooped them up one at a time to lie against her. Sunlight streamed through the windows, much brighter than dawn, and she glanced at the alarm clock across the room on the floor.

"I slept in, boys. No wonder you were working me over. You must be starved."

Still groggy from a late night of watching and worrying, Laura trudged to the laundry room, poured cat food into the double dish and gave the kittens fresh water. In the living room she combed her fingers through her tangled hair and stood at the window. Life at the ranch was right on schedule. Sprinklers stretched silvery arms across the pastures, geese squatted sunning by the pond, cattle grazed. The golf cart tooled down a dusty lane, and Eli came to mind.

She recalled the gun shots.

Had he really fired at rustlers last night? Or the cougar? A marauding coyote? A skunk? Garcia said he wouldn't actually shoot someone, but would merely shoot *near* them. She scanned the pastures below. No dead bodies, as far as she could tell.

Keeping a promise to herself she pulled on shorts, a tank top and her running shoes and headed out the French doors.

The hill awaited—a steep half-mile descent of chewed-up asphalt and potholes.

At the bottom she turned south, toward the narrow S-curve and long straightaway bordering the ranch. A covey of quail flushed across the road and into the underbrush. Doves *coo-aahed* from cottonwood trees, and the sprinklers swished out a steady background beat. Laura raised her face to the sun, relished its warm caress and started out at a slow jog. Oh, how she'd missed the country.

She jogged past the ranch and along a sheltering row of ash trees. In the pasture a dwarfed oak spread an umbrella-like canopy, evenly trimmed where cows had stretched their thick necks and nibbled the edges.

Coming toward her, another runner hugged the same side. She slowed to a walk and stepped into deeper shade for the runner to pass. And then she recognized her.

"Mary?"

The woman stopped and leaned against her knees. "Hi." She heaved a deep breath. "Do I know you?"

"Laura Bell. I met you last week at your store."

Mary straightened and smiled. "You have a good memory." She stepped off the road and into the shade and bent to wipe her brow on her shirttail. "So you live out here, on Campbell Creek?"

"Up on the hill there." Laura pointed back to the first ridge that overlooked Hawthorne Ranch.

"Wow. You must have a great view."

"I do."

"So you run, too."

Comparing her dry skin to Mary's sweat-drenched body, Laura couldn't exactly call what she did *running*. "Sort of. I jog, really. But I'm hoping to work up to it. It's been a long time."

"I remember you said you were starting over."

"In a lot of ways."

Mary stooped to tighten a shoelace and Laura thought back

to their first meeting. "I found a snicker doodle bread recipe and it turned out pretty good."

Mary nodded and addressed the other shoe. "I'm not surprised. After you left that day I finished off that mini loaf all by myself."

"You live very far up the road?"

The woman stood and flapped her shirttail like a fan. "A half mile past the mailboxes, first drive on the right. Would you like to run—or jog—with me some morning?"

Encouragement seeped into a hidden corner. "I wouldn't want to slow you down."

Mary pulled her ropelike braid over her shoulder and wrapped her hand in it. "Don't worry about that. I'd enjoy the company. Though I usually leave a little earlier. Got a late start this morning."

"What time?"

Mary flipped her braid back. "That's your lane across from the mailboxes, right? What if I meet you there tomorrow at six? Before it gets too hot."

Mary obviously didn't sleep in. "Sounds great."

"Good. See you then."

The woman smiled and jogged away, her braid bouncing against her back as she picked up her pace.

Laura walked on beneath the sentinel ash trees, a spark of anticipation growing into hope. A possible friend. And a healthy one at that. Mary was closer to her mother's age, but the woman could outrun her with little to no effort. Exactly what Laura needed. A friend *and* motivation.

After a quarter mile she turned toward home with a new sense of direction—and on impulse cut through the fence onto the ranch. She wouldn't have to run all the way back to the road to get home. She could slip through the back pasture. Like she had as a kid.

For a moment she was twelve again, running down the road searching for Eli and a new adventure. She stopped, smoothed her shirt, tucked her hair behind her ears and took a deep breath. She was not a child. Some decorum was in order. At a more leisurely pace, she strolled into the central yard bordered on three sides by outbuildings and spotted Eli hooking a spray rig to a four-wheeler.

He must have heard her for he spun quickly, challenge written on his face in the split second before recognition. His shoulders relaxed and a slow grin lifted one side of his mouth. He adjusted the eye patch and leaned against the quad, arms folded on his chest.

"Hey, Laura Bell—"

She stopped. Jammed her fists on her hips. Glared.

Raising his hands in surrender, he laughed. "All right, all right. No ding-a-ling." His full-blown grin told her his concession came at a high price. She thanked him by unballing her fingers and assuming a respectable demeanor.

"Looks like you're in attack mode." She nodded at the white tank attached to the quad.

He pushed away from the fender. "Yeah. Should have done this earlier, but other things came up."

"Like rustlers?"

The grin vanished, replaced by defensiveness.

She noted his clenched jaw, the tightening of his bare forearms. A soldier, she thought. Ready to fight. She glanced at his left leg. No different than the other.

"I heard gunshots last night," she said.

At her abrupt confession, his gaze slid to the upper pasture. He lifted his hat, ran a hand over his hair. "So you did." He jammed the hat on and his features hardened. "I missed."

A chill swept through her. She stepped closer and softened her voice. "I thought you were *supposed* to miss." He met her eyes and held them long enough for her to see pain etched in the beautiful blue-gray.

"Man or beast?" she ventured.

His lips curled in that new unsettling way. "Both." He regarded her briefly, then climbed onto the quad and reached for the ignition.

She moved closer and touched his shoulder. "Eli."

He flinched, whether at her fingers or her voice she didn't know, but she desperately wanted to reach the *other* Eli. A bold idea flashed through her mind. "I'll bring dinner tonight."

He turned his spotlight gaze on her, probing her intentions. "You got any more sweet bread?"

A small sigh escaped her lips. "Absolutely." Mentally she scoured her cupboards for the ingredients. "I thought I'd make enchiladas." She hadn't thought about it at all. "And rice."

"I've got a can of beans in the cupboard."

Relieved, she parried with him. "That's probably *all* you have in your cupboard. You certainly don't have anything in your refrigerator. What have you been living on?"

He tugged on his hat brim, started the quad and threw one word at her.

"Fish."

Laura watched him drive down the central lane and slow at the first paddock. He reached back for the spray wand attached to a hose and spread a fine mist into the ditch along the fence line. The distinctive odor of weed killer drifted her way and she turned for the upper pasture.

Traipsing through tall grass in tennis shoes and shorts invited a snake bite this time of year. Keeping an eye on the ground ahead, she crossed the pasture, slipped through the red pipe fencing and stopped by the Miracle Tree. Garcia was right. Both she and Eli needed a healing touch. Something had burned a hole in Eli as surely as the fire that gouged this tree.

"Can You use me, Lord?" She stooped to peer inside the hollow shell, and wondered if her own healing would come when she reached out to another wounded heart.

Chapter 9

Eli released the spray lever, crossed the intersecting lane, slowed and aimed the nozzle at the next ditch line. He twisted around to see if Laura still stood by the tractor shed.

Gone.

An awkward jolt tipped him to the right as the front wheel ran into the ditch. Jerking the handlebars, he corrected and resumed a straight path paralleling the fence line.

That's what he got for letting distractions pull him away from the task at hand.

A beautiful distraction.

One that planned to show up tonight with dinner. His mouth watered at the suggested menu. Had she remembered enchiladas were his favorite, or was that merely a coincidence? And what was her motivation? Friendship? Morbid curiosity? Evangelism?

He could use a friend, but he didn't need a preacher. So far she hadn't pressed the prayer issue, but if she ganged up with Garcia, things could get ugly. And he didn't know if he could just be a friend. Something about her pulled at him, filled him with longing for more than what they'd had as children. Taunted him with possibilities of what they could share as adults.

What if she didn't want the same? What if his scars repulsed her? What if she played the God card?

Clicking off the nozzle, he laid it across his lap and cut a U-turn at the lower pasture. He eased over along the opposing ditch, grabbed the nozzle and started in on the return trip.

Garcia walked out from the buildings, a coiled rope in his hands. His wide-brimmed palm leaf hat resembled his *vaquero* forefathers' sombreros. Aside from the brown chink chaps he wore, short and fringed at the knee, Garcia could easily pass for an early *Californio* landowner. And why not? Half of Hawthorne Ranch belonged to him.

Eli found the transaction shortly after Pop's funeral, the first time he justified the books. Rather than feeling run under, he felt relieved to know Garcia's interest focused on more than merely a job. But Eli couldn't understand why his old friend wouldn't move into the main house.

Maybe he liked his privacy.

Or maybe he didn't want to share a roof with someone who refused to pray.

Eli rolled to a stop and shut off the engine.

"So, my friend, you left early this morning." Garcia built a small loop and flicked his wrist to set it spinning.

"Ate at the coffee shop. Hoped to hear news about rustlers."

"And you did?"

Eli removed his hat and rubbed his forehead. "Not a word. Place was quiet. So was the feed store."

Garcia raised his head until his dark eyes appeared beneath the wide brim. "I heard your rifle in the night."

Eli nodded. "One man on horseback." He grinned. "But not on his way out."

Garcia smiled appreciatively, dipped his head, twirled the

flat loop. "I saw nothing during my watch. Maybe the *coyóte* will not return."

"I wouldn't count on it. All I did was let him know we're on to him. Now he'll be more careful."

"We watch again tonight?"

"At least until moonrise." Eli clapped his hat on, pulled it low on his brow.

"I will take the first watch."

"Then don't eat too much or you might fall asleep on a full stomach."

Garcia looked up, a question in his eyes.

"Laura's cooking. Enchiladas."

The older man's face split in a pearly grin. "*Bueno*. She is good for us, no?"

Eli glanced at the hill. "We'll see." He started the quad and Garcia stepped back. "Meet me in the bottom pasture and we'll pull sprinklers."

Garcia's palm leaf dipped in answer and he dropped the loop, pulling it into the coil before heading for his pickup.

Laura dragged herself up the front steps, through the French doors and leaned against the refrigerator while ice water filled her glass. She'd covered a lot more ground than originally planned this morning. How had she ever managed to run these hills as a kid with Eli?

Eli. The more she thought about him the more she wanted to crack through his chameleon cover. Of course he wasn't the gangly teenager she'd shadowed as a preadolescent. But she wanted to know what had molded him over the past dozen years. What had cut him so deeply to leave a cold, steely edge in his eye? Why did he react so defensively?

She rolled the chilled glass against her face and neck and grudgingly admitted that Mary Travers was right about running early in the day. And she had fewer than twenty-four hours to recover enough to meet the woman at the bottom of the hill tomorrow morning.

A quick shower rejuvenated her, and as she pulled on capris and an embroidered white peasant blouse, she mentally tallied ingredients for enchiladas. A flan might be fun, too. And she'd buy extra refried beans. No telling how long Eli had had that can. His granddad may have bought it.

She checked the front lock, grabbed her purse and keys and opened the French doors in time to see Pennington ride up her driveway on his pitiful buckskin.

Great. What could he possibly want? She needed to leave if she wanted to make the trip to town and back and still have time to do all the baking. But something told her not to drive away while he hung around.

She eased the door closed and dropped her purse on the counter, unwilling to let Pennington know she planned to leave.

After tying his horse to her mulberry tree, he lumbered up the steps and knocked.

Laura thought about not answering but her car gave her away. She opened the door a few inches.

"Yes?"

Pennington removed his sweaty felt hat and smiled. "Hello there. Do you have a moment?"

So much for efficiency.

"Just one."

His smile never changed and she thought it appeared more sinister than friendly.

"On your way out?" He swept her attire with a hungry gaze.

"What do you need, Mr. Pennington?"

He glanced over his shoulder at two patio chairs on the deck. "I thought we could visit for a bit, since we're neighbors again and all."

Couldn't this guy take a hint?

"Especially since we might have trouble in the area." He squinted one eye as if waiting for that last remark to sink in.

An icy shiver slid down the back of her neck. "And what trouble would that be?"

His smile vanished at her refusal to come outside and a cold, hard glare replaced it.

"Did you hear gunfire last night?"

Laura knew she was a terrible liar. Mama had seen to that. But she didn't want to tell him she'd heard Eli shoot at rustlers. Twice.

"I heard a mountain lion." She held his stare. "Do you think someone shot at it?"

His right cheek twitched and he looked down at his hat.

"It's awful dangerous having someone out here shooting in the dark. Could hit a cow or something they didn't intend." His eyes shifted to hers without his head moving.

"You're absolutely right," she said. "Did you ask anyone else who lives around here?"

He shoved his hat on. "No, ma'am. Not yet. Thought I'd start with you."

He nodded and walked down the steps, then turned to face her. "You be careful now—up here all by yourself."

His words ran like spiders up her arms and she tried not to slam the door as she closed it. She turned the lock and stepped back from the glass door as he untied and mounted the buckskin. As if he knew she watched, he looked toward the French doors and touched a finger to his hat brim—the typical cowboy goodbye.

Except Ken Pennington was anything but a typical cowboy.

Shopping took Laura's mind off her creepy neighbor and forced her to think about cooking—which she enjoyed and Eli didn't appear to do much of. In addition to cheese, onions, olives, enchilada sauce, Spanish rice and refried beans, she bought fresh vegetables, extra tortillas, eggs, chorizo sausage and milk, plus everything the two men would need for hamburgers other than meat. Surely Eli had a freezer full of beef. And fish.

One pan of enchiladas should give the men two meals, a second pan she'd tuck in the freezer, and Eli could grill burgers after that. Settling on a boxed flan, she hoped Garcia wouldn't mind that her caramel-flavored pudding wouldn't be home-made like his mother's.

At the mailboxes she crossed the road, eased in close and reached for the black one.

Empty.

Why did she keep checking? If Derek had anything to say, he'd email her. She hoped he wouldn't. There was no point. Everything had been said.

Checking her mirror for traffic, she pulled out and across to her lane. Thick knee-high grass covered the hill from the fence and on over the crest. It hadn't been grazed in years, and dry lightning this summer could spell trouble. She needed cows. Four or five to graze it down. She shoved the car into gear and quickly climbed to the top and into her driveway's sharp right turn. Pennington and the buckskin stood atop the next hill, a hundred feet above her. Watching.

Up here all by yourself.

She shuddered, cranked the steering wheel and accelerated around to the end of the house.

On Pennington's side of the barbed wire, bare ground stretched like thin, dry skin. No fire threat there. His white-faced Herefords had always reached through the old fence for Bell pasture. It didn't take much for them to push through. Daddy would let them eat for a few days. Felt sorry for them, he'd said. Then he'd herd them back through the gate.

Laura felt no such pity for Pennington or his cattle. The man should know better.

She hefted her groceries inside and mulled over the prospect of running cows again. Maybe Eli would sell her a few of his dry cows, mamas whose babies were stolen. She'd mention it tonight at dinner.

Chapter 10

Eli rubbed his face and head with the bath towel, feeling naked without his patch. Only when he slept or showered was the strap not snug around his head.

He retrieved a new one from his dresser, slipped it on and hopped to the closet for a chambray shirt. Blue used to be her favorite color.

Would she notice?

Garcia's head was hidden by an open cabinet door when Eli descended the stairs.

"She is here." The older man set three plates on the kitchen table. "And the beer is cold."

Eli chuckled. The "beer" was Garcia's way of welcoming Laura home—dark, sweet, chilled root beer like they'd had when she and Eli were kids.

"I could use some help here." Laura stood peering through the back screen door, a casserole dish in each hand. Eli hurried to let her in and took one dish.

The warm aroma of fresh enchiladas surrounded her like

perfume. "This smells great." He took in her long, straight hair and embroidered summer blouse. "And you *look* great."

"Thank you. On both counts." Sliding her casserole in the oven, she turned the dial to warm. "Put that one right here. After it cools completely, we'll freeze it. That way you two men will have another meal later in the week."

Garcia nodded. "You are good to us, *Lorita*."

"I have to be. I saw how you two eat the other night." She beckoned to Eli. "There's more in the car. Give me a hand?"

He followed her out to the sleek convertible and mentally calculated how many calves he'd have to sell to buy a car like that.

"Can you get these two without spilling?" She handed him the smaller serving dishes, and her teasing concern brought back memories of how they once bantered.

"You doubt my abilities?"

She puffed out a laugh and hefted a grocery bag. "Of course I do. You're a man."

"Same ol' Laura Bell, you ding—"

"Don't even." She pushed the passenger door closed with a hip. "When it comes to cooking, you fry a mean fish. But I looked in your refrigerator and cupboards. So don't give me any grief."

She held the screen door open and stepped aside. "Just smile, nod and say thank you."

He did.

From the bag, Laura retrieved lettuce and several tomatoes. "*Abuelito,* will you chop these for us please?"

"*Si, mija.* You make me remember my own mother's house."

"Well, I can't make tortillas like your *mamá,* but I can heat these." She plopped a bag of flour tortillas on the counter and turned to Eli.

"There's one more thing in the car I forgot. Will you get it, please? It's in the trunk. Push a lever under the steering wheel to open it."

Glad to have something to do besides standing around trying not to look at her, Eli returned to the car and popped the trunk. A plastic-wrapped pie plate of flan sat encircled by a large towel. As he reached in, he noticed a pair of black heels shoved in a corner—those weapons disguised as shoes on the first day he saw her. Hard to believe the woman in his kitchen was the same slicked-back starlet he'd kept from falling in the ditch.

He balanced the plate on one hand and slammed the trunk. Laura Bell had baggage he knew nothing about. Something she was trying to kick free of.

Just like him.

Her laughter floated from the kitchen as he entered the back porch.

"Garcia, you old sweetheart! I love you forever."

The man's eyes twinkled as she kissed him on the cheek.

"What's he up to now?" Eli set the flan in the refrigerator.

"Root beer." Unmistakable delight edged Laura's voice as she gestured toward the table. "Look at this—chilled glasses and everything."

Definitely not the aloof city girl from the other day. This was Laura Bell in all her country glory.

Goldie padded in from the family room and plopped down under the table with a sigh.

"Now you've done it." Eli stooped to rub the yellow head. Woke the watchdog."

"She smells enchiladas, no?" Garcia grinned and placed a dish of diced tomatoes and chopped lettuce on the table.

Eli grabbed a salsa jar from the refrigerator and noticed the chorizo and several other new items. "What's all this?"

"That's known as food, Mr. Hawthorne. I imagine you have ground beef. You can grill hamburgers after you and Garcia finish the enchiladas. The chorizo is for breakfast burritos."

He stuck a spoon in the salsa and took his place at the head of the table. She was thinking about him. A good sign.

Laura and Garcia took their respective seats. She folded

her hands in her lap and looked at Eli. He gritted his teeth and nodded at Garcia. The old man bowed his head.

"*Gracias, Señor,* for this food, and the land and these young people."

Laura's head remained bowed a moment longer and when she looked up, her lashes were moist. Reaching first for the server, she dished out enchiladas. Everyone helped themselves to beans, rice and tortillas, and for several minutes a contented silence settled over the kitchen.

"I want some cows." Laura took a long, slow drink from her root beer, leaving fingerprints on the chilled glass as she set it down.

"Cows?" Eli met her gaze.

"*Si. Vacas,*" Garcia said.

Eli shot him a look as he chewed. "You've nearly got 'em with Pennington's herd reaching through your fence every day."

Laura shivered and jerked her head to the side. Eli's internal warning system flared. "What's he done?"

She sighed and cut into her enchilada. "He hasn't really *done* anything, other than come by the house a couple of times."

The way she said it put Eli on edge.

"I don't want his stock on my place." She laid her fork on her plate. "I know that sounds petty, but I'm not as generous as my dad was, letting those scrawny things graze a few days before he drove them back through the gate." She took a bite of beans, glanced at Garcia, then looked directly at Eli.

"Would you sell me some?"

Garcia spoke first. "Why not take a few of our dry *vacas*. They eat the grass and cry for their *becerros.*"

"I had the same idea, but I want to pay for them."

Eli considered arguing with her, but he knew she'd sull up and kick back. "Two hundred a head."

Garcia choked on his root beer.

"What is it?" Laura shifted her gaze from one man to the other.

Garcia wiped his mouth. "Too much and too little."

"And I'll throw in labor to repair that fence between you and Pennington," Eli said, hoping to distract her from his ridiculously low quote.

Laura twirled a fork in her refried beans. "I've been thinking about that. Who built your pipe fence?"

Eli tipped his chin at Garcia. "We did, with Pop. Why?"

"How much would it cost to run pipe fencing from your property line to the top of my drive?"

Pennington really was getting to her. Eli crumpled his napkin on his plate and pushed it back. "It'd be cheaper—and just as good—to use cable and pipe. Steel pipe for the posts and top rail, and cable for the rest of it."

He watched her face as she considered his suggestion. Never one to give in to his ideas without a tug-of-war, she frowned and dug furrows through the beans on her plate.

"I'll figure it up and let you know," he said. "If that's what you want to do, we'll need to start as soon as possible, before the grass dries enough to catch a welding spark."

Laura laid her fork down, reached across the table and clasped his arm with one hand and Garcia's fingers with the other.

"Thank you. Somehow I knew you both would help me." Misty-eyed again, she scooted her chair back. "And I have a surprise. Hopefully, it's as good as the two of you."

Eli's stomach turned at the remark. Garcia might be good, but him? He was anything but good, and as soon as Laura found that out, she just might hightail it back to the city.

She brought the cold flan to the table and scooped large helpings onto small plates.

"Ah, *Lorita,* you are kind to my old heart." Garcia's smile brightened his face.

"Not to mention your stomach," Eli said.

They all laughed and Eli savored the creamy, carameled pudding, tasting, as well, the richness of Laura's presence in his home. In the past few days, he and Garcia had laughed more than they had in the past year.

If only he could be good. Good enough for her.

That evening Eli dug through his closet for a small wooden box he'd made in high school woodworking class. He found it on a shelf under several pair of holey jeans. Smoothing his hand along the top of the box, he sat on his bed and raised the hinged lid.

As always, the right side of his face twinged when he looked at the Purple Heart, and a phantom pain shot through his left foot and ankle that weren't there. Below the medal lay several envelopes.

The first held his formal discharge papers, the next his grandfather's death certificate and obituary. And beneath that, lay a small square envelope with LAURA BELL block-printed on the front.

He cringed, remembering his decision to print her name. At fourteen, his cursive stank.

He pulled out the folded paper and memories fell around him—the unexplainable ache in his chest when he learned she'd be leaving. His sadness over her father's death, the things he wanted to say and couldn't. Not even in writing.

At the time, he'd justified his cowardice by thinking he'd wait for her new address. But he never learned her new address. Never heard from her again. Never got rid of the letter.

With a man's eyes he read a fourteen-year-old boy's words:

I wish you didn't have to go.

Come back again.

Eli Hawthorne III

In the day's fading light, for a long, painful moment, he questioned which had been worse—the day the roadside bomb blew him out of the Humvee or the day Laura moved away.

Chapter 11

Laura cocooned herself in the quilt on the front porch swing, wondering where Eli waited on this moonless night. Or would Garcia take the first watch?

Eli had been right again about the late rise, and the ranch laid dark and silent, the buildings barely distinguishable in the starlight.

He'd worn a blue shirt at dinner which brought out the blue in his eyes. Funny, but she would always see him with two eyes, in spite of the bold, black patch.

Above her to the east, Pennington's outside light glared over his house, barn and the granite boulders jutting from the hillside. He, too, could be sitting on his porch, watching the valley, a rifle across his lap.

She shivered.

Soon Pennington's cattle would no longer push through her fence. She tugged the quilt tighter. Why hadn't her dad fixed that fence years ago? Didn't he have the money?

There had been so much love in her family and so little

money—one reason she'd been drawn to Derek Stone. She exhaled a shaky breath.

She'd thought she'd found both love and money when she fell for the handsome, successful banker. He'd been so taken with her.

But being in love wasn't the same as loving, and soon another attraction took him away.

The ache began behind her breastbone, throbbing slowly. She blamed her hasty decision as much as she blamed him for his unfaithfulness.

Unwilling to spoil the day with post-traumatic pain from her former fiancé, she went inside and locked the door.

The next morning, common sense told Laura to drive the half mile down the hill and park at the edge of the lane. Who knew how far she'd be going with Mary, and she might die if she had to walk back up after their run.

Pride won and she walked.

The sun had barely glazed the cottonwoods as she took to the lane, and on the north face a few late wildflowers clung to the shady spots—purple fiesta, popcorn and the delicate white blooms atop the platelike leaves of miner's lettuce. Overhead a woodpecker thrummed against a steel telephone pole, and she marveled at the bird's dedication to a hopeless endeavor.

A shadow slipped through her mind. Was she doing the same, trying to chip through Eli Hawthorne's tin-man armor?

She shook off the depressing thought and quickened her pace. At the bottom she waited across from the mailboxes, unwilling to further darken her mood by checking hers and finding it empty again.

Mary appeared around a bend, her long strides bringing her steadily closer.

"You made it." Mary greeted her cheerfully with an outstretched hand.

Laura was glad she hadn't driven. At least she'd stretched

her legs out a little. "Thanks for inviting me, but I have to warn you, I'm in terrible shape."

Mary gave her a quick once over. "Not really. No extra weight. You'll do fine. Probably just need to build up your lungs."

Laura inwardly winced with a long-held desire to build up more than her lungs.

Mary was kind. They jogged down to the Hawthorne Ranch gate, about a mile, and then headed back. Laura could feel those inadequate lungs screaming for relief, but she forced herself to keep up with her merry mentor. Not only could the woman outrun her, but she talked while she was at it.

"What's it like coming back after such a long time?" Mary looked straight ahead, waiting for Laura's reply.

"Different." If she could stick with one-word answers, she might survive.

"I can imagine. We moved here from Oregon a dozen years ago. Never looked back. Rich wanted to live here ever since visiting as a kid. Crazy, I thought. Oregon is hard to beat, but I've grown to appreciate the beauty here, though it isn't as green in the summer."

"I'll bet." Two words.

"He's retired, but not me. I run the store and he runs errands." Mary looked Laura's way and smiled. "I imagine there are more homes around here than when you were growing up."

"Absolutely." One word.

"The valley that opens past the next couple of curves is a well-kept secret."

"Hmm." No word.

"We love it here."

They were nearing her lane, and Laura prayed she could keep jogging until they got there. Without falling down.

Mary slowed to a walk and Laura nearly hugged her. Sucking in as much air as possible, she lagged only a half step behind the older woman. At the mailboxes, she stopped and leaned on her knees.

"You did great, Laura."

She turned her head sideways to see Mary's generous smile. "Thanks."

"You want to meet tomorrow, too?"

"Sure."

Mary laughed and lightly patted Laura's back. "You're a trouper. It'll get easier, I promise. See you tomorrow."

Laura straightened and nodded. "I'm counting on it."

As Mary jogged off toward home, Laura thought she might throw up. She eyed the lane snaking up the hill and considered trudging down to the pond instead and throwing herself in.

The sour note of a gate hinge rolled up from the ranch, and a horse whinnied. If Eli and Garcia could see her now, they'd laugh her to scorn.

No—Garcia wouldn't laugh. But Eli would howl.

The climb took less from her lungs but more from her legs, and by the time she limped up the porch steps, Laura knew spaghetti had replaced her bones. She flopped onto the sofa, too weak to answer the furtive meows coming from behind the laundry room door.

Tomorrow she would drive down.

She must have dozed off, for a drawn-out feline snarl woke her with a start.

"I'm coming." Pushing herself to a sitting position, she took a deep breath before standing. Her legs were less rubbery and hope surfaced that she would, indeed, live another day.

Pete and Re-Pete dashed from confinement and skittered through the kitchen.

"If I had your energy, I'd be invincible."

The kittens trotted through the house on the hunt for any excuse to play.

After a shower and fresh clothes, Laura felt like herself again. She put in a load of laundry, gave the carpet a cursory run with the vacuum and sat down to check her email.

Eli dismounted and led Buddy and an older mare through the north gate and onto Bell property. Then he rode a diagonal line up the hill to fencing just below the house. Pleased with his surprise, he stopped in front of the barbed wire separating Laura's yard from the pasture. He'd waited until after nine, giving her time to shower and do whatever she did every morning. If she'd stayed true to her younger leanings, she'd be outside digging something up.

He stood in the stirrups and stretched his thigh muscles. The saddle creaked as he settled against it, and the mare whinnied impatiently.

He'd been counting on that.

The front door opened and Laura stepped onto the covered porch. He tipped his cowboy hat and lowered his voice with his best Western gentleman's accent.

"Mornin', ma'am. Nice day for a ride to Slick Rock, wouldn't you say?"

A smile slid across her face as she folded her arms and cocked her head to the side.

"You're awfully sure of yourself, Mr. Hawthorne. Or do you always bring a spare mount along when you're out riding?"

Buddy stomped a hind leg and lipped at the sweet grass hugging the fence line.

Laura looked past him to the bottom land. "How'd you get in here?"

"No lock on the gate down at the west corner."

"I might have to fix that." She tossed a visual challenge his way. "Looks like I've got more than the neighbor's livestock trespassing on my property."

He reined buddy away from the fence and turned him downhill.

"Wait!" Laura jumped off the porch and hurried to the fence. "I'll go."

He pulled his horse around and eyed her cutoffs and pink tank top. "Not like that, you won't."

"Give me five minutes." She slipped under the porch railing.

"Don't forget a hat, Miss Bell."

Waving a hand over her shoulder, she disappeared inside.

Laying the reins against Buddy's neck, Eli turned back to face the ranch. He marveled again at how pristine it appeared from a distance. Tracing a line from the east pasture where the rustler had been and up over the draw, he saw how easily a rider could make a clean getaway. If he figured right, the rodeo grounds lay below the ridge on the other side—a perfect place to hold calves before trailering them out unnoticed on a moonless night.

Anger simmered under his skin as he tallied the money he'd lost to rustlers. He planned to take a closer look today when he and Laura came back from the waterfall.

The screen door slap jerked his head around. Laura wore a ball cap with a long ponytail hanging out the back, jeans and tennis shoes—not safe for a ride. He'd have to remedy that. A fair payback for all the groceries.

He stepped off Buddy and over to the fence where he stepped on the bottom wire and pulled up on the next strand. Laura slipped through the opening without snagging her shirt and moved around Buddy toward the mare.

"Easy, girl," she murmured, running her hand down the mare's neck toward the saddle.

Eli handed her the reins, and she deftly gathered them and grabbed the saddle horn. With the other hand she took hold of the cantle, did a little half hop, then jumped, catching the stirrup with her left foot. She swung her right leg over the mare's rump and settled in.

"Bet you thought I forgot that trick."

He nodded. "Looks like I was wrong. How are the stirrups?"

She stood on the balls of her feet. "Just right. Good guess."

"Good memory," he said, and turned Buddy downhill toward the gate. Laura hadn't gained much height in the past twelve years, so he'd let the stirrups out one notch.

"No boots?"

"No need." She threw him a side glance. "Until today."

"Well, as long as she doesn't run off with you, you'll probably be all right."

She wrinkled her nose at him—that childish face she'd thrown his way a hundred times when he'd been right and she didn't want to admit it. He chuckled.

At the gate, he rode through first and closed it after her, then they turned toward the hills at a slow steady pace, side by side.

No trail led to the falls, other than the memory of their frequent hikes to the giant granite slab. The horses picked their way along the grassy slopes, effortlessly climbing a couple hundred feet that would have left Eli and Laura panting. The animals' bobbing heads set a steady rhythm that rocked the world away.

As they topped the next hill, Slick Rock lay below them, shimmering white in the morning sun. Washed smooth by centuries of rain and runoff, its broad, bare face hugged the eastern side of a watershed. Only in the spring was it an actual waterfall.

Eli pointed his horse down a gentle slope and stopped in a narrow flat place on the rock's southern edge. He dropped the reins and Buddy lipped at the grass, twitching his ears and swishing his tail.

Laura dismounted and hugged the mare's neck, cooing something soft in her ear.

Eli climbed onto a wide slab of bedrock pocked with bowl-shaped hollows several inches deep. Laura joined him, sat down cross-legged between two holes and ran a hand around the smooth insides of one.

"Heck of a way to grind acorns," she said.

"Not for the Yokuts." Thanks to Pop, he knew the Native Americans had roamed the foothills long before Hispanic farmers and ranchers moved in.

"It's just like I remember." Laura leaned back on her hands and gazed at the dry waterslide. "I hope people don't build around here. I'd hate to see that great blank face marred with graffiti."

"Belongs to the Bureau of Land Management. Probably won't ever be built on." He hoped.

"Mary Travers told me there are quite a few homes farther up the road. Back in the little valley past those curves."

He nodded. "City people who want to live in the country—including a highway patrol officer. Nearly everyone commutes to work. Not many ranchers."

She studied him a moment. "Are you and Pennington the only cattlemen left up here?"

"No. And don't count Pennington in the bunch. He's no cattleman." He took his hat off and set it upside down on the rock.

Her silence accentuated his scorn.

"Gillette still owns a lot of the foothills," he said. "Old family, if you remember."

"I remember the name."

"They drive their cattle higher in the summer and back down to the valley before the snow flies. One of the few remaining cattle drives in the area."

A sudden sadness tinged her voice. "We can't stop change, can we? Go back to the way things were."

His lip curled when she mentioned his inner turmoil. "Nope."

She looked squarely at him then, her dark eyes clear and questioning. "If we could, what would you change?"

Her boldness surprised him. He'd thought age would have tempered her brash, straight-forward manner. It hadn't. Any more than it had his.

He stuck his left boot out and pulled up his pant leg. "This, among other things."

She didn't flinch, didn't gasp or shrink back in horror. Just stared at the prosthesis connecting boot and leg.

What had he expected? Pity? Revulsion?

Again she surprised him with a bold appraisal.

"Doesn't look like it's slowed you down any."

He grunted, pulled his pant leg down. "I manage."

"I suppose you'd change everything that happened in Afghanistan."

"Wouldn't you?" He glared at her. What did she know about ambush and pain beyond description?

She dipped her head, took a deep breath and let it out slowly. "Yes, I would."

Guilt knifed his gut. He hadn't intended to assault her with his self-pity. He tried again. "What would you change about your life?"

"My mom would be alive." She answered without hesitation. Then she paused, looked at the mortar holes pocking the slab. "And I'd change some of my choices—decisions I made that didn't turn out so well."

He nodded, remembering her remark about coming close to marriage. He wanted to know what happened, but like he'd said before, it wasn't any of his business.

"You never married?" She beat him at his own game.

"No." He watched her run her fingers around the inside of a mortar. "Never came close."

"I did. Came close, I mean." She stared at the bedrock. "But I picked the wrong guy."

He couldn't help himself. "What happened?"

"A week before the wedding, he picked someone else." She dropped her head as if ashamed.

Anger surged through his arms at the gesture, and his fingers curled around the throat of an imaginary idiot.

The question spilled out before he could stop it. "Why didn't you write?"

A short gasp escaped her parted lips, and surprise drained the color from her cheeks.

"I'm sorry," he said quickly. "You don't have to answer that." He grabbed his hat and slammed it on. "I didn't mean for this to be a depressing ride."

As he gathered himself to stand, she reached to stop him.

"It's not depressing. And I'm glad you asked the question. It's one I asked myself for a long time, and I think the answer has to do with pain."

He relaxed and tipped his hat back, sensing she had more to say.

She crossed her legs, wrapped her fingers around an ankle and looked at the slide.

"I didn't want to leave. This was the only home I'd ever known. I loved it here."

She paused, swallowed. "And my best friend lived here."

Her best friend? He didn't remember her ever talking about her school friends, and the two-year difference in their ages had put them in different buildings with different schedules. He didn't see her much at school.

In a near whisper she added, "I didn't want to leave him behind."

Eli's heart bucked and his muscles tensed. A learned response. He willed himself to stay seated and calm.

"I was afraid that if I wrote, you wouldn't write back, and that would have been more than I could bear."

He tried and failed to dislodge the gravel in his throat. "I would have written."

She faced him with a sad smile. "It's kind of you to say so."

He thought of the note in the wooden box on his dresser, realized he was a lying coward. He *had* written her.

Taking a deep breath, she straightened her back, lifted her chin. "So I filled my life with school and helping my mother. Good grades led to scholarships which led to a teaching degree."

"That doesn't sound so bad."

"It wasn't." She stretched her legs out and leaned back on her hands. "My Afghanistan was opening myself up to the wrong man." Honesty blunted her expression and she fixed him with a steady gaze. "My scars aren't as brutal as yours, or as life-altering. But they've changed me in ways I don't like."

His throat tightened at her show of courage. "You haven't given up."

She reached for his hand. "Neither have you."

He wrapped his fingers around hers and tugged. She scooted

closer, into his arm, and leaned against him. The top of her cap rubbed under his chin and her shoulder lay warm against his chest. Could she feel his heart pounding?

A hawk screed and drew his attention to its spiraling rise above them. Once it reached its flight point, it tilted off toward higher ground, its broad wings spread wide against a blue backdrop.

She relaxed against him, watching the bird. "They ride the thermals, you know."

"Hmm." He ran his hand over her shoulder, feeling the softness of her, breathing in her sweet scent.

"The heat carries them as it rises." She said it as if trying to convince herself of something she didn't quite understand.

"All they do is spread their wings."

She stiffened, sat up, wonder on her face. "That's it!"

"That's what?"

"That's what I couldn't figure out."

"You couldn't figure out that they spread their wings?" Was he missing something?

Suddenly she retreated, withdrew inside herself, and the mood between them shifted. What had he done?

"It's nothing." She tugged the ponytail over her shoulder and combed through it with her fingers. "Just something I've been thinking about for a few days, that's all."

"Want to share?"

A door closed on her beautiful brown eyes, and the sad smile returned.

"Maybe when I understand it better myself."

Frustrated that he'd shattered the moment, he cleared his throat and got to his feet. "Hungry?"

She sighed, seemingly relieved at the change in topic. "How'd you know?"

"I'm a good guesser, remember?"

If he was such a good guesser, why couldn't he guess what he'd done wrong?

He hiked back to the horses. Ground tied, they grazed where

he had dropped their reins. From a saddlebag he retrieved an aluminum foil bundle and two water bottles. Then he led Buddy to another spot, dropped the reins again and did the same for the mare.

When he returned, Laura stood at the edge of the bedrock mortars, hands in her back pockets, staring at a small creek that trickled below them.

"Breakfast is served."

Chapter 12

Laura returned to their spot, stepping between the mortar holes, and sat down next to Eli. "Isn't it a little late for breakfast?"

"For me, yes," he said. "I ate at about five-thirty. These are leftovers." He unwrapped the foil and spread it on the rock. "Chorizo burritos. Your idea."

"Absolutely. But I thought you and Garcia would eat them all."

"You bought two pounds of chorizo. It'll take us a while to get through that."

She bit into the tortilla-wrapped roll of sausage, egg and potato. "Mmm."

With a pleased look on his face, he did the same.

"Not bad," she said with an honest nod. "I'm impressed. I thought you only did fish."

"You kidding? I learned everything I know about the kitchen from Garcia."

"That's what I said."

He laughed and nudged her with his elbow. "Don't let him hear you say that. He'll put jalapeño juice in your root beer."

Laura covered her mouth, choking on a vision of Garcia holding his finger against floating jalapeños as he tipped juice from a jar. She wouldn't put it past him—even if he did love her like a granddaughter.

Eli had caught her off guard with his question about writing, and she'd surprised herself with her admission. In all those years of tagging along behind him, she'd not thought of him as her best friend. But time's filter clearly defined his role in her young life. She'd fairly worshipped him—and just as often hated him. A fine line there.

He'd taken her confession well, and she dismissed the embarrassment that tried to wiggle under her skin. She hadn't expected to tell him how she'd felt when she and her mother moved away, but his question deserved an honest answer. What a pair they were—both wounded and wrapped in the past.

Oh, God, help us.

She'd heard the thunder of his heart when he pulled her close. Uncertainty? Longing? His gentleness as he stroked her shoulder suggested the latter, but right now she wanted only his friendship. She needed more time to heal.

The water cooled her throat, and she drank half the bottle before capping it and wadding her foil.

"Another?" Eli offered a burrito.

"No. I'm stuffed. Save them for Garcia."

"He ate three this morning."

She shook her head. "I believe it. He sure puts away his share for such a wiry guy."

Eli pulled his hat brim down and stood. "I want to ride over the ridge behind the ranch before we head back. You game?"

She gathered the remains of their breakfast. "I'm game."

Eli offered her a hand and pulled her up, sweeping her face with a blue gaze. She squeezed his fingers before releasing her grip, but he held on.

She aimed for a lighthearted tone, but it snagged in her throat.

"What is it?"

"I'm glad you came back," he said softly.

She'd seen that look on a man's face before and fear pulled her head down. The bill of her cap blocked his approach.

"Me, too," she murmured.

He hesitated and she held her breath. A quick squeeze of his fingers, like a benediction, and he let go and started for the horses.

She followed, watching his broad back, the swing of his arms, the fit of his jeans, the slight hitch in his step. She noted, too, the hitch in her pulse. Their relationship had deepened, shifted gears. Become more.

The climb to Slick Rock had been familiar, but now Eli rode over another hill and into new territory. From the ridge she could see their valley—all of Hawthorne Ranch and beyond, and her house perched on its lower knob to the north.

Captivated by the view, she reined in the mare. "It's beautiful."

Eli stopped beside her. "Sure is." He crossed his arms on his saddle horn, the same position he'd taken the day she first saw him.

"Do you ride up here much?" she asked.

He scanned the scene below them, turning his head slightly as he looked to the right. "Not enough. Wasn't the same without you." A half smile slid across his lips and he turned Buddy away to plod along the ridgeline.

Laura touched the mare's sides with her heels, urging her into a trot, and Eli's words slipped into the empty place at her core.

After a short ride around another hillside, he stopped at the top of a low saddle-shaped dip in the hills and faced east, away from their homes. She pulled up next to him and recognized the Spring Valley rodeo grounds below.

"I think the rustlers are running my calves over this draw

and down to the holding pens," he said. "Then trailering them out."

"How can you be sure?"

"I can't. Not until I catch them red-handed."

"How will you do that?"

He looked at her and a chill as cold as creek water ran down her back. "Next time, I'll be waiting for them."

At the fence line in front of her house, Laura dismounted and handed the reins to Eli. "Thanks for taking me."

His earlier sinister look had vanished, replaced by the easy-going, lopsided smile. "My pleasure, ma'am." He dipped his chin in a brief nod.

"You don't have to get down—I can manage the fence." To prove her ability, she slipped through two barbed wire strands and faced him from the other side. "Let me know about the pipe fence and when I can get the cows."

Eli leaned on the saddle horn. "You've got twenty acres, right?"

"Right."

"I'll run in four or five. How's that?"

She smiled. "That'll be great. Thanks. I'll write you a check."

"No hurry." He turned the horses toward the bottom land. "I know where you live."

"Wait."

He stopped, twisted in his saddle.

"Does this make me a cattlewoman now?"

He grinned and shook his head. "Not without boots."

He angled the horses across the hill and down toward the gate where he dismounted, walked them through and left it open behind him.

Laura slipped beneath the porch railing and watched until he disappeared over a low rise and out of view. In a moment, she saw him again, heading for the barn. He left the mare and rode back to the upper pasture.

He cut five head from the bunch and at an easy pace drove them north toward her open gate. She marveled at the way Buddy worked the cattle, cutting off the leader in its attempt to turn back at the gate. Lured by the deeper grass, the others followed and immediately bent their heads to graze.

She pulled off her cap and shook out her ponytail. Eli raised a hand after shutting the gate and she returned his wave, smiling to herself. Not only would she be a cattlewoman—regardless of what Eli said about boots—she was also going to be one very *sore* cattlewoman tomorrow morning.

That evening Laura soaked in a hot bath, hoping to head off achy muscles from the ride. She hadn't been on a horse in a dozen years. Hadn't been fishing. Hadn't seen such breathtaking views, and hadn't realized that Eli Hawthorne III would take her breath, as well.

She was beginning to feel like her old self, but she didn't want to plough into something she might regret.

Old self? Her mother would laugh and tell her she didn't know old.

Her throat constricted. Mama hadn't known, either. Forty-seven wasn't old, but cancer respected no one's age.

Pete and Re-Pete trotted into the bathroom and tussled on the bath mat, lightening her mood. She flicked water from her fingers and laughed as they twitched their whiskers and looked around for the source.

After drying off and donning her cutoffs and tank top again, she sat on the sofa with her laptop and searched for information on cattle rustlers.

Rustling on the Rise in Western States, said the headline to the first article she read. The writer blamed a slumping economy for an increase in the activity once considered cause for hanging. Idaho, Colorado, Montana, Nevada and Wyoming had the highest incidents, and often thieves rode in on four-wheelers. A silent crime, the report said, with losses in the millions of dollars.

Another article reported ranchers in Texas and Oklahoma also suffering, and thieves were often employees or neighbors. She learned what Eli meant by running a brand, and saw images of running irons used to modify the distinctive markings on livestock.

Refining her search, she typed in "cattle rustling in California." The news was just as bad. Especially for owners who didn't brand their cattle, like a lot of dairymen.

She closed her laptop and tried to remember the Hawthorne brand. A simple H. Easy to change, based on what she'd read. The whole thing sounded like an old-time cowboy movie, but evidently stealing cattle was as prevalent as knocking over a liquor store. Easier, if the thief knew what he—or she—was doing.

Which meant most rustlers knew how to take care of their target. Most were cowboys or close to it. She immediately thought of Pennington. Eli scoffed at the man's abilities, but Pennington certainly knew enough to heist a few calves from a neighbor and drive them over the hill to the rodeo grounds.

What would Eli do if he caught the man doing just that?

She didn't want to know.

In answer to her growling stomach, Laura made a cheese, lettuce and tomato sandwich, sliced an apple and took the meal and her Bible out to the front swing. As she ate, she thumbed through Isaiah for a verse she'd once read about eagles.

A breeze danced across the porch and she looked up to see a thin cloud cover. Lying low and golden on the eastern horizon, the sun spotlighted the lesser hills with a bright yellow wash and sent long shadows over the Hawthorne pastures. In minutes it slipped away and the land lay down with a sigh, at rest in the shadowless dusk.

The breeze kicked up and a hushed, breathy sound rasped against the mulberry leaves. Soon the whisper swelled and spread to the roof. Heaven opened and rain fell over the house like a veil, soaking the pastures and trees. Her cows stood unbothered in the deluge.

Laura rose to stand against the railing. She breathed deeply and stretched her hands beyond the eaves. Lightning struck across the valley and thunder quickly followed. Two miles away, at most.

She peered through the grainy dusk to the spot where the Miracle Tree stood anchoring that corner of her land. Anchoring her soul with hope. She walked to the end of the porch and down the steps into the rain.

"I get it, God. I finally get it."

Closing her eyes, she spread her arms like the hawk, lifted her face and let her tears mingle with heaven's cleansing shower.

Eli stared through the rain toward Laura's house. From the opened barn door the steady downpour on the corrugated roof sounded like distant automatic weapons fire. Four years ago he wouldn't have made the connection. Now everything made a connection.

Laura hadn't flinched when he pulled up his pant leg—a stupid thing to do, now that he thought about it. She'd taken the shock and tossed it back in his face. Was she just acting tough, stiffening in defense against anything he threw at her? Like she used to?

Tugging his hat down and his collar up, he strode to the house. Water gathered in the brim and trickled off the front edge. He stomped into the back porch, shook off his hat and slung it on an old set of longhorns Pop had mounted above the coat rack. For an Angus breeder, it was the closest thing to horned cattle he'd ever have.

Leaning against the wall with one hand, he toweled off his left boot, then pulled off the right one with the boot jack. Sometimes he forgot about his leg—until he kicked off a boot or shoe and padded across the floor with one sock-covered foot and clomped with the other. The truth eventually surfaced: he wasn't all there.

He and Garcia had devoured Laura's enchiladas, and he

pulled the second pan from the freezer and slid it in the oven. He opened a can of refried beans, set them over low heat on the stove, then called Garcia from the desk phone and told him dinner would be on in a half hour.

The old man must have let Goldie in the house before the rain started, because he caught a glimpse of her on his way upstairs, stretched out on her side before the fireplace. Chasing geese.

Crazy dog. A warm, summer evening, in spite of the rain, and she stuck to her spot as if it were winter.

At the dresser he lifted the box lid and stared at the blocky, boyish print on the square envelope. Would their lives have turned out differently if he'd sent Laura the note? What would she do if he sent it to her now—laugh at him or be offended? Again he felt her soft warmth against him as they sat on the bedrock. He'd nearly kissed her when he helped her up, and she evidently knew it, for she'd ducked her head just in time.

Maybe it was too soon.

He dropped the lid and headed for the bathroom.

Showered, changed and starving, Eli trotted down the stairs to the distinct odor of scorched beans. Garcia stood at the counter salvaging what he could into a serving bowl.

"I had it on low," Eli said as he pulled two plates from the cupboard.

"But for how long?" Garcia shook his head. "No *Lorita* to sit at our table tonight?"

Eli had thought the same thing but didn't want to admit it. "She doesn't want to eat here every night."

"How do you know? You have not asked her."

Eli grabbed a towel and pulled the bubbling enchiladas from the oven. "I'm sure she has plenty to keep her busy up there on her hill."

Garcia tossed a pot holder on the table and it slid to a stop beneath Eli's poised dish.

"Good shot." He grudgingly acknowledged the older man's ability to read his thoughts. Garcia's sixth sense was a comfort when it came to running the ranch. But sometimes Eli felt the man could look into his chest and see his heart beating.

"De nada."

Eli sent Garcia a sidelong glance as he took his seat. "I ran five head into Laura's bottom land from our north pasture today."

Garcia nodded and scooped two enchiladas from the pan to his plate. "We have enough pipe to run to her hilltop. I will start tomorrow."

"Good." Eli savored a mouthful of tortilla-wrapped onion and melted cheese. "Shouldn't take more than a few days to finish. Then she won't have to worry about Pennington's cattle pushing through."

Garcia nodded again.

Since his grandfather's death, Eli hadn't cared that little conversation or laughter accompanied their meals. But Laura's return and recent presence at their table had brought life back to the ranch house.

Tonight, without her, the silence hung heavier.

Chapter 13

Five forty-five came quickly but not quietly, and Laura forced herself across the room to the alarm clock on the floor and into the bathroom. The insides of her thighs told her this morning run thing wasn't such a great idea.

By five fifty-five she had driven down the lane and parked in a turnout just off the main road.

She leaned against the car, palms on the fender and stepped back, lunging on one leg and then the other. Her thigh muscles screamed in protest and she considered telling Mary she'd have to cancel.

A disgustingly cheerful "Good morning!" squelched the idea.

She looked up to see the woman a few yards away. Fresh and strong and healthy as an Olympic athlete. Laura wanted to throw up.

Mary slowed to a walk and stopped at the car, concern on her face. "You sore?"

"I went riding yesterday and I'm paying for it today."

"O-oh." Mary stretched out the word and shook her head. "That'll get you every time. How long since you rode a horse."

"Would you believe twelve years?"

"Ouch." Mary cupped one elbow, and pulled her upper body around in a side twist. "How about if we walk today? Sound good to you?"

Embarrassed but grateful, Laura agreed. "You wouldn't mind?"

"Not at all. Just so I'm moving." She did a few side bends and flexed her knees one at a time. "Besides, you don't want to do any serious damage. Walking will be good for you. Work out the pain."

Laura struggled not to roll her eyes. "I hope so."

"Tell you what. Let's walk to my place and I'll fix you a cup of my special tea blend for sore muscles."

Laura glanced at her car. "Sure you wouldn't rather ride?"

Mary laughed and pulled her long braid over her shoulder. "No. You need to walk. Come on." She started out. "It's not that far. About a half mile."

Laura groaned inwardly but refused to wimp out on her neighbor's kindness. "I'm right behind you."

Mary shortened her stride as they took to the paved road. "How many horses do you have?"

"None. I went riding with Eli Hawthorne."

"I've never met the man, but what a gorgeous place he has. I hear he was a marine. Injured in Afghanistan, if I remember."

"Yeah. He lost an eye." A sudden image of his steely-blue gaze flashed in her mind and she felt warm all over. "And his left foot and ankle."

"Oh, my." Mary looked at her feet. "I can't imagine what he must go through."

Laura smiled to herself. "He pretty much does everything he always did."

Redwing blackbirds and larks sang in the new light, and as morning stretched across the meadows, the pain in Laura's legs eased from a sharp burn to a dull ache. Mary had been right. Walking helped.

At the next bend in the road, a short lane cut off to the right and ended in a tangle of trees and shrubs. Laura hadn't ventured this far north since her return, but she vaguely remembered a sprawling ranch-style home in this general vicinity. She followed Mary through a break in the overgrowth and discovered that it served as a privacy hedge. Clever.

A breezeway split the low structure—a covered, tile-floored area that connected a two-car garage to the main house. Mary took a door to the left and they stepped into the kitchen where a large gray cat lounged on an antique dining table. From a short hallway ahead came the distinctive bay of a basset hound that steamrolled into the room.

"Welcome to the circus," Mary said, stroking the overweight tabby as she passed by the table. "Buford, say hello to our new neighbor, Laura Bell."

Buford complied and showered Laura's legs with a slobbery shake of his jowls.

"Have a seat," Mary said as she filled a kettle with tap water. "Just push Theodore out of your way if he bothers you. I don't know what it is about the table that he loves. The tile floor is just as cool as the oak tabletop. Cooler, I think."

Laura seated herself one chair over from Theodore's silky mass, and ran her hand along his side. "Maybe he likes being up high where he can see what's going on."

Buford planted his stubby self beneath the table's edge, tilted his head back and dragged two, long barks from his throat.

"Hush, Bu."

At Mary's sharp rebuke, he looked once more at the cat and trotted back down the hallway and out of site.

"He's jealous." Mary took two mugs from the cupboard and placed a tea bag in each one. "He thinks Theodore gets special treatment."

Laura chuckled and stroked the rotund feline. "I have two kittens. Hopefully, they'll turn into good mousers."

A large window above the table revealed a grassy yard that sloped toward Campbell Creek. A fallen cottonwood, whitened with age, lay across the creek bed like an invitation.

"You have a lovely place," Laura said.

Mary set a bright blue mug before her and took a seat across the table. "Yes, I've come to really enjoy it." She looked out the window. "Deer often drink at the stream, but in the spring they also help themselves to the bulbs in my garden. I don't enjoy that so much."

Laura sipped the hot tea, trying to detect the herbs in Mary's sore-muscle remedy. "I don't have any critter visitors, living on a hilltop like I do." A sudden image of Ken Pennington flashed through her mind and she nearly corrected herself.

Mary set her mug on the table and absently feathered her fingers through Theodore's fur. "Did you know Eli when you were growing up?"

Laura smiled at the memory. "Yes. We grew up together. At least for a few years—after my mother let me out of the house alone. I guess we spent five or six summers just being kids— swimming, fishing, climbing trees, riding calves."

Mary's brows popped up. "Riding calves?"

Laura laughed. "Once they were weaned, I'd help Eli corner a calf then he'd jump on its back and ride until he fell off."

"Did he ever enter the rodeo in Spring Valley?"

"He finally talked his granddad into letting him enter the kid's steer riding. Wanted to ride bulls, but Mr. Hawthorne wasn't too crazy about that." She took a longer sip, rolled it around in her mouth. "I don't know if Eli ever convinced him, because I moved away right after my twelfth birthday."

Mary leaned back against the chair and cupped her hands around her mug. She regarded her guest with an easy, open acceptance, and Laura felt oddly comfortable. As if she could tell Mary anything and not be judged.

"We've lived here almost as long as you've been gone,"

Mary said. "Rich loves it, as I told you the other day, and it's finally become home for me, too." She sipped the tea. "So where were you living before you came back."

Laura turned her eyes to the window and her thoughts inward. "With my mother. My fiancé bought and furnished what was to be our new home—a condominium—and I was moving my few things in a piece at a time."

The throbbing began, but she pressed on, feeling safe with Mary.

"On one of those occasions I surprised Derek." She looked at her new friend who sat calmly listening and sipping.

"With another woman."

Mary's cup halted in midair and her eyes flickered.

"I simply left. No big scene. Just took what I could carry and left everything else. Including his ring."

"Was it a total surprise or had you suspected something?"

Mary's question forced her to look at the truth. "I think I suspected. I think that's why I didn't tell him I was coming, just showed up."

The throbbing eased and she returned her gaze to the window and the fallen cottonwood. "When Mama died I brought her home, took our place off the market and decided to give myself a year to heal and start over."

Mary nodded. "I remember your purchases that first day at the store."

Laura swirled the tea in her mug and nodded. "The most fun I'd had in a year."

"Well I'm glad you picked our store." Mary reached across the table and squeezed Laura's hand. "I hate to break this up, but I need to get ready for work."

"Oh, I'm so sorry." Laura scooted away from the table.

"Not to worry. I just need to stick to my schedule or I'll be late. We'll have to do this again." She smiled in her warm, accepting way, and Laura believed she meant what she said.

Setting her cup in the sink, Laura thanked Mary for the tea. "Do you carry this brand at the store?"

"And several other herbal varieties. Next time you're in town stop by and I'll show you."

With one final rub of Theodore's more than ample torso, Laura let herself out the side door and headed for the main road. What a hideaway Mary had. As reclusive as her own hilltop.

She took to the pavement and silently thanked God for bringing her home to a new life and a new friend.

And to Eli.

Her insides fluttered. An undeniable response to the mere thought of the man.

Laura parked beside the house and walked down to the corrals to check the water tank. She should have done that before letting Eli run those cows in.

Weedy grass filled the pens, long vacant and unused, but when she turned the spigot, water gushed into the tank. She climbed over the pipe fencing and swung all the interior gates back against the rails. Hopefully her cows would mow out the pens.

The corrals sat on a lesser hill that jutted out west of her house. From here she had a broader view of the county road that ribboned through the valley and past Mary's place. She located the roof of Mary's long rancher, the trees and shrubs that sheltered it from the road and several other homes built since she'd left. The hill country definitely had more houses than before. More change. But good change, she decided. What if everything remained the same? Wasn't growth what life was all about?

Splashing water told her she'd let the tank run over, and she hurried to shut off the spigot. She had chores now, and the thought pleased her. Animals depended on her to care for them—animals besides Pete and Re-Pete.

What about people? Eli in particular. Would he ever need her?

The flutter returned, and experience cautioned her to not

get her hopes up. But he'd told her he was glad she'd come back. Wasn't there hope in that?

A black head bobbed over the crest of the hill, followed by four others. The cows crowded around the tank, slurping noisily and wiping their noses with long, slick tongues.

She laughed out loud at the familiar scene she'd long forgotten. What else about ranch life had she let slip away?

The question sent her to the shed that butted against the corrals—her dad's storage area where he kept his tools and other supplies. The door opened easily and stretched cobwebs across the frame. She found an errant branch and cleared them as she stepped inside. Speckled light filtered into the dusty cavity and most of what had once been there was gone. She scanned the workbench, looking for traces of her former life, expecting to find little if anything.

At the far end an old mailbox sat in rusted neglect with a piece of wood attached to the front flap. Laura gasped, remembering the bright yellow bell that distinguished their box from the others at the road. She rummaged among stray bolts and odd iron pieces until she found a discarded straight-edge screwdriver. With it she loosened the screw that held the wood to the box, and twisted a nut off the backside.

A little sanding and a splash of fresh paint and the bell would be good as new.

Chapter 14

Eli helped Garcia load pipe and welding supplies into the stock trailer hitched to his pickup. He tossed a shovel in the pickup bed, lifted Goldie in, then slid behind the wheel.

Garcia took the tractor with the auger attached to the back and opened the upper gate between the ranch and Bell property. He drove through and waited for Eli to bring the trailer around.

Parking parallel to the sagging barbed wire, Eli estimated it would take thirty posts from his pipe fence to Laura's driveway, about two hundred yards altogether. Pennington's cattle watched from the other side, resting in the shade of an old oak.

He lifted Goldie from the back, scoped the pasture for his—Laura's—five head and found them trailing down from the corrals. Didn't matter where the water lay, livestock could always find it. Smelled it, Pop had told him. The very thing that often caused stampedes on those long cattle drives in the 1800s. Cattle could smell water more than a mile away.

Laura's wave from the top caught his eye, and he returned

the signal. His heart rate climbed a notch at the sight of her. Even from a distance she was beautiful.

Goldie bedded down in the pickup's shade while Eli and Garcia worked on the first section. By midday, ten steel posts sprouted along the old wire fence, and Garcia had a good start on the top rail. Eli pulled off his hat and wiped his shirt sleeve across his forehead as Garcia raised his welder's mask.

"Siesta," Garcia said.

Eli nodded, unhitched the trailer and cranked the jack foot down. Then he, Garcia and Goldie took the pickup back to the ranch house.

After lunch and a gallon of iced tea, Eli relaxed at his desk, pulled up the feed store's website and scrolled through for clothing. They didn't have much, but he remembered seeing a boot display when he'd stopped in the other day. A good women's work boot was all he needed. Nothing fancy. No bling.

Laura would have to try them on. He reached for the phone and realized he didn't know her number. No doubt she had a cell phone, so he couldn't look it up. He hadn't thought to ask her. Guess he'd have to drive up and ask her now.

Hmm.

Garcia had stretched out on the old leather sofa and Goldie occupied her favorite spot by the fireplace.

"I'll be back shortly," Eli said from the doorway to the family room.

A ceiling fan stirred the air and Garcia raised a hand. Goldie chased a goose.

Laura's land bordered his, her house looked down from the first hill to the north, yet he had to drive all the way down his lane, out to the pavement and a mile up the road to get to her turnoff. He needed a shortcut.

Slipping through the S-curve, he again recognized its danger. On the first half, the road crested. The northbound lane curved to the right, the southbound to its left. If a driver going either way failed to hold his lane and met oncoming traffic at the top, the resulting crash would be a dead center head-on. Eli's grip tightened on the steering wheel.

He rarely drove through the curve, but Laura did every time she went to town. Which from the number of times her sports car shot by, was plenty. When school started, she might be driving it even more.

Topping the rise, he spotted Laura's car parked off the road on the right. She stood across the pavement at the mailboxes attacking one with what looked like a screwdriver. He pulled in behind the convertible and watched.

She glanced over her shoulder with a scowl and returned to her assault. As far as he could tell, the only thing she was accomplishing was improving the tan on her slender legs.

"Want a hand?" he offered as he stepped from his truck. He crossed the road and took a closer look at her project.

Laura pressed a yellow bell shape with a long screw against the front of her mailbox. Her other hand wielded an ancient screwdriver that was no doubt the source of her scowl.

He frowned, forcing a spontaneous smile from his lips.

"Let me see that."

She glared at him.

"Please let me see that." He extended his hand and hoped she wouldn't shove the straight edge through his palm.

With a huff she slapped the screwdriver in his hand and held out the yellow bell. "I found this in the shed this morning and took it off our old mailbox."

He caught the distinct odor of new paint.

"If I took it off that one, why can't I get it on this one? It's not brain surgery."

His mouth quivered, jerked from a smile by military-strength resolve. "Your dad probably drilled a hole in the metal before he attached the bell. Was there a fastener on the backside?"

Comprehension washed across her features and she dropped her head. "Yes. I have it right here." She fingered a small rusted nut from a front pocket and held it up.

"I've got a drill," he said. "Wait here."

He turned and gave in to a soft chuckle, allowing his lips to relax in a smile. From his truck-bed toolbox he retrieved a cordless drill, and then reached deep for a solemn expression.

"You've made a dent in it," he said, looking closer on his return. "Is that where you want it?"

"Yes."

He drilled a quick hole, she held the bell in place and he pushed the screw through and into the metal. She threaded the fastener on and finally stepped back looking relieved.

"Thank you," she said, fixing him with her dark eyes. "You have great timing."

He raised the power drill. "And the right tools."

She conceded with a grin. "Guess I need to go shopping again."

"That's what I came to see you about."

She accompanied him to the truck. "Really?"

"Yeah. I want to get you a pair of boots." He returned the drill to his toolbox.

Her cheeks flushed and she dipped her head a fraction as she looked away. "You don't have to do that. I can afford boots."

He eyed her car. "I know you can. That's not the issue. I'd like to repay you for all those groceries and for reminding us what good food tastes like."

She laughed under her breath.

"As a matter of fact, Garcia thinks you should be so generous every night."

Her eyes flew to his as if looking for more.

"I told him you had better things to do than feed a couple of busted-up cowboys."

Disappointment flicked across her face. "I enjoy it," she said. "It gives me something to do."

"Well, we enjoy it, too. I enjoy it."

She smiled then, as if finding what she was looking for.

"So when do you want to go boot shopping?" she said.

"I'd like to put a couple more hours in on your fence today, but we could take off about four. Hit the feed store before it closes."

"You want me to meet you there?"

"No. I'll come get you. But I might not have time to shower before we go, so I could be a little gamey." A lot gamey was more like it.

Grinning, she pocketed her hands. "Not a problem, cowboy."

He slid behind the wheel and noticed his cell phone on the console. "I nearly forgot, what's your number?"

He entered it in his phone and hit save. "You don't have a landline, do you?"

"No. I don't really need one."

On a small notepad he kept in the glove compartment he wrote two phone numbers, tore out the paper and handed it to her.

"The first one's the ranch line, second one is my cell."

"Thanks." She folded the paper and tucked it in her back pocket.

He started the engine, rested his arm on the opened window.

"Thanks again," she said. "I was really about to lose it when you stopped."

He pulled his hat up, smoothed his hair back, tugged the brim down. "My pleasure, ma'am. See you about four."

Laura entered Eli's numbers in her cell phone and taped the paper to the freezer door with a pleased tap. Her first piece of refrigerator art. Then she went to her closet to decide what to wear to the feed store.

She giggled. Feed store? Derek would puke in disgust.

After a quick shower, she pulled on a pale blue peasant blouse with an embroidered yoke, jeans, thick socks and tennis shoes. She dried and curled her hair, applied blush, mascara and lip gloss, and for the first time in a long time, smiled at herself in the mirror.

"I have a date."

She giggled again at the hilarity of the situation and sought out the kittens who were taking a midday nap in the living room beneath the ceiling fan. She compared their tiny bodies to Theodore and found it hard to believe they were remotely related. Mary must spend a fortune on cat food.

She poured ginger ale over ice, sliced an apple and cheese and took the meal out to the porch with her laptop and checkbook. She set the glass and plate on her most recent find, a small square table next to the swing, and used her computer as a writing surface. Her first order of business: a thousand-dollar check to Eli Hawthorne. She tore it from the checkbook, folded it in half and slid it into a back pocket. After all her research about rustlers, that figure seemed more like what she should pay for a couple of calves, not five full-grown cows.

She had no idea what he'd charge for the pipe and cable fencing, so that check would have to wait.

Reaching for the ginger ale and plate, she gave the swing a little shove to set it rocking. Eli and Garcia worked in her pasture. Occasional sparks winked around Garcia's Ironman-like mask, and the occasional clank of Eli's shovel against steel announced the lengthening boundary. He was right. He'd be ripe after a day of hard labor beneath a hot summer sun. At least they had the auger to dig the post holes.

Just after four she heard his diesel engine chug up her driveway. She grabbed her keys, locked the French doors and hurried down the porch steps. She didn't want him to see her empty house. Like it mattered.

Except it did.

"Sorry I'm late." He smiled and his teeth seemed whiter in the midst of a day-old beard.

A whisper of shower soap lingered in the truck, and a clean shirt and jeans gave him away. So much for the rank cowboy. Laura wondered if he had more in mind than the feed store.

"Late doesn't count unless it's church or school." She buckled the seat belt and looked at her tennis shoes. "I wore thick socks, based on what I remember about my last boots."

"Good plan." He kept his eye on the road that wound down her hill and once on the pavement, gave her an appreciative once-over. "You look great. But you always look great."

She inhaled slowly through her nose, determined not to blush. "Thanks."

"Were you sore this morning?"

She huffed out the breath. "You're kidding, right? I could hardly get out of bed."

Laughing, he shook his head. "I figured you would be, but you're not limping or walking like a bowlegged cow puncher."

His smile infected her with a giddy fever and she rolled down her window. "I walked this morning to Mary's, and she served hot tea that she promised would relieve sore muscles."

"She ought to know. I see her running down the road nearly every morning."

"We're supposed to be running together, but I couldn't today."

He turned right at the T, then left onto the main highway into Spring Valley. "You'll get your riding legs back."

"I know. I just have to keep moving, keep from getting stiff."

As Eli increased his speed, her hair whirled around her face. She clasped it in her right hand and leaned her elbow on the doorframe.

"We can run the AC if you want."

"No—I like this."

An odd expression pulled at his mouth and she couldn't see his left eye as he watched the road. But the space between them filled with a familiar comfort, and she felt like she belonged there beside him.

Only two vehicles sat in the feed store lot, one of them a flatbed truck backed up to the loading dock. A tall slender cowboy tossed several feed bags onto the bed and finished with a chunky, pink salt lick. The customer shoved the bags against the front frame and secured them with bungee cords.

Eli glanced at the employee, frowned as he exited his pickup and tugged his cowboy hat down low on his brow.

Laura followed him through the front door.

The smell of hay and grain and leather jerked her back across the years, and she inhaled deeply. Nowhere but in a feed store would she find such sweet perfume.

The wall to her left held an opened bay door, and the skinny cowboy ambled in from the loading dock. She wasn't touching Eli, but she was close enough to feel his tension. He focused on the back of the store, and in a deep, quiet voice said, "This way."

The employee watched them with a smirk as he pulled a thin, round box from his shirt pocket, pinched out a dark wad and stuck it in his lip.

Laura concentrated on looking elsewhere and exhaled in relief when Eli stopped before a boot display. Styles had certainly changed since she was a kid, and nearly every boot had a squared off toe and fancy stitching on a short, boxy top. But a tall red pair at the back with a high undercut heel caught her eye, and she thought how fun it would have been to make an appearance at one of Derek's office parties in those boots and a short denim skirt.

"What are you thinking?" Eli said quietly.

"I'm thinking of a place I would like to have worn these." She lifted one red boot and checked inside for the size.

"I thought you wanted to be a cattlewoman."

She glanced at his worried expression and chuckled. "I didn't say I wanted them *now*."

Returning the boot, she scanned the others for something more durable with a work feel to it.

Eli handed her a brown bull-hide boot with a lower heel and an ornately stitched red leather top. "How 'bout a compromise?"

"Oh, yes." Pleased with his choice, she sat down on a low stool and untied her tennis shoes. "They're too small," she said, tugging on the straps.

"What size do you wear?"

Laura peered inside the boot. "These are a five. Do they have a six?"

Eli ran his hand down the stacked boxes under the display and pulled out the fourth one from the top. The picture on the end matched the boot.

"Perfect." Laura stood and rolled onto the ball of her foot to check for room at the heel. She remembered what her dad had told her about fitting boots.

"Here, try them both." Eli pulled out a cardboard form and handed her the other boot.

She pulled it on and walked a few paces down the aisle and back again. From the corner of her eye she saw the cowboy nodding at her, and she thought she heard him say something about a filly to another guy at the cash register. They both snickered.

The look on Eli's face told her he'd heard the comment, too.

She touched his arm, forced him to face her. "These are perfect."

He looked at her but didn't see her. His attention fixated on the lanky guy at the counter.

"Can I wear them out?"

"Sure." Eli stuck her tennis shoes in the box and closed the lid. Then he headed toward the front with slow, fluid steps. Like a cougar about to pounce.

The other employee rang up the sale, and the smirking, tobacco-chewing fella brought himself and his fat lip around the end of the counter. As he did so, he scanned Laura's body with an irreverent leer.

"Now there's a filly I'd like to try."

Eli's body tensed and Laura saw his jaw clench. He returned his credit card to his wallet, his wallet to his back pocket and faced the mouthy man with a deadly glare.

"Whoa, there, Hero Hawthorne," the cowboy said, both hands raised in surrender, but no such sentiment in his eyes.

"Can't fault a guy for checking out the merchandise, now can you?"

Laura touched Eli's arm and felt steel beneath his sleeve.

"You owe the lady an apology."

The smirk widened. "Really? And how do I know she's a lady?"

Eli's right hand struck like a cobra. His grabbed the man's shirt and yanked him up until only his booted toes scraped the floor.

White-faced with panic, he clawed at Eli's hand.

"Now you owe her two."

The clerk behind the counter moved toward them and Eli stopped him with an icy glare. "Eli," Laura whispered.

He ignored her and bore into the defenseless man's face with his cold, blue eye.

"Sorry, ma'am," the cowboy choked.

"That's one," Eli said in a clear, tight voice.

The man's eyes darted to Laura and back to his captor. "No harm intended, ma'am."

"Two." Eli uncurled his fingers and the man dropped like a feed sack. Tobacco juice oozed from one side of his mouth as he backed down the aisle toward the exit.

Laura stood immobilized, staring.

"That was uncalled for, Hawthorne." The kid at the cash register stepped out of Eli's reach.

"Was it," Eli said, no question in his tone. He cupped Laura's elbow and gently turned her toward the door.

Chapter 15

Eli eased his truck out of the feed store parking lot and toward the main part of town.

"I'm sorry." He had to fully turn his head to see Laura sitting close to the passenger door. "But I couldn't let him talk to you like that."

The boot box lay on the seat between them. It might as well have been a granite wall. She stared straight ahead, her hands folded tightly in her lap.

His plans for dinner at the Burger Barn drained away, along with any thought of getting closer—until she spoke.

"No one has ever come to my defense."

The quiver in her voice made him want to go back and hit the guy. Hope flared to a tiny ember.

"If I hadn't called him out, he would have mouthed off even worse."

"You've had a run-in with him before, haven't you?" By the sound of her voice he knew she'd turned her head toward him.

He nodded and signaled left at the Burger Barn. Parking

in front, he killed the engine, punched his seat belt free and twisted around in the seat to face her. The maneuver increased his frustration over having just one eye.

"You tensed when you saw him on the loading dock, and again inside," she said.

Her dark eyes searched his face with no rebuke.

"Instinct. Backed up with a few facts." He laid his right arm on the seat back, his fingers inches from her hair. "He's a womanizer, a liar and a punk."

One corner of her mouth twitched and an eyebrow arched and quickly straightened. She'd never make a good poker player.

"How do you know?"

"He claims to have earned several commendations for valor in Afghanistan. I called him on it the first time I ran into him."

"What makes you doubt his word?"

"Because I've seen guys like him before. All talk and no tank. All hat and no cattle." He pulled his keys from the ignition. "And Garcia said the guy came back six months before me, full of brag. Didn't get enough attention, I guess."

"And you got a newspaper story."

He stared through the windshield at the red-and-white checked curtains framing the Burger Barn door. He'd go somewhere else to eat if he could.

She reached for his hand and turned it over.

His heart shifted into high gear and sweat popped out above his hatband.

"Just checking your fingers," she said, stroking his palm. "I wouldn't want you unable to finish the fence because you felt you had to defend my honor."

The tension in his shoulders drained away at her playful remark. "Gee, thanks," he answered with mock offense.

"Thank *you*." She squeezed his hand.

Her tenderness and genuine gratitude pushed him to the edge of a place he hadn't been in years, and he grappled with his emotions, fighting for equilibrium. "Hungry?"

Laughing outright, she let go and unfastened her seat belt. "You do have your priorities, don't you?"

"Of course. This place has the best burgers in the state. And their fries aren't bad, either."

She leaned forward and tucked the bottom of her jeans into her boot tops. "But do they have root beer floats?"

"You buying?"

"Only cows. If the boots didn't break you, I imagine you can afford dinner, too."

She slid out her side.

He held the diner door for her, then motioned toward a booth in the far right corner. Taking the side against the wall, he sat in the center rather than inviting her to sit next to him. If Tobacco Breath followed them, he wanted to see the door before she did.

Laura scooted onto the opposite seat and reached for the menus tucked behind a white enamel bucket holding mustard, ketchup and napkins.

"What'll it be, Hawthorne?"

The cook's abrupt holler startled her and she jerked around in her seat.

"It's Toby, the owner. He always does that," Eli said, reaching across the table for her hand. He saw her visibly relax, and guessed she was still on edge from the feed store incident. "I'm going to yell our order back to him, okay?"

Laura took a deep breath and eased it through her lips. "Sure. But you don't know what I want yet."

"Yeah, I do."

Without releasing her hand he leaned away from her and raised his chin. "Two cows with a stack o' hay. No cheese."

She giggled and whispered, "Don't forget the root beer float."

"And two beers with cream."

"Comin' up."

She was watching him with one of those mixed looks he

remembered from their childhood. Questioning. Admiring. Challenging.

"This place too fancy for your blood?"

Her mouth curved into a perfect smile. "This place is perfect for my blood."

She pulled her hand away, reached into a back pocket and pushed a folded paper across the table. "For the cows."

Without looking at the check he slipped it in his shirt pocket. "Thanks. Now I don't have to charge you interest."

She wrinkled her nose at him.

The owner delivered two glass mugs of foamy root beer with bobbing scoops of ice cream. "Two beers with cream," he said, placing one on either side of the table.

"Thanks, Toby." Eli nodded at the aproned man. "Laura, this is Toby McClure. Toby, Laura Bell."

"Hello, Toby." She offered her hand. "You have a great place."

Bald but amply mustached with a fine handlebar, Toby wiped his hands on his apron and took hers with a brief shake. "Thank you, ma'am. Gotta keep up appearances for famous people like Eli, here."

Eli cleared his throat and jerked his head to the side in a send-off. "Don't burn our dinner with your yakkin'."

Toby grinned and thumbed over his shoulder toward the wall as he left.

"What's that all about?"

"He likes to keep his customers entertained." Eli pushed his ice cream down with a spoon and stirred, hoping she wouldn't look too closely at the wall. "So how do the boots feel?"

"Great." She spooned off a bite of ice cream and a white smudge stuck to her lip. "Mmm, even greater."

He pulled a napkin from the bucket, and poised it halfway across the table. "May I?"

She cocked her head to the side, a question bunching her brows.

Leaning forward he dabbed her mouth.

With a disgusted little grunt, she snatched the napkin and wiped it across her lips. Her dark eyes danced with laughter.

"Good grief, Eli," she teased. "You pick out my boots, pick out my food and now you're picking at my face."

"Somebody's got to take care of you."

"I can take care of myself, thank you very much. I'm a grown woman."

No kidding. That bit of information had not failed to imprint on his heart. "And a fine one at that, I might add."

Her cheeks flushed and she dropped her gaze, spooning off another bite.

"What if that guy at the feed store presses charges against you?" she said.

Her sobering question raised issues he didn't want to get into. "He won't."

As stubborn as the twelve-year-old he remembered, she pressed the point. "What makes you so sure?" She scraped the crystalized edges from her ice cream.

"Because he's not going to admit he was bested by a cycloptic cripple."

Her spoon stopped halfway to her mouth and she stared at him. "Is that really how you see yourself?"

Now it was his turn to break eye contact. The conversation was not going the way he'd planned.

The spoon slipped from her fingers and clanked on the edge of her glass. She fixed him with a hard look. "You're not defined by your injuries, Eli Hawthorne. We all have scars, wounds, handicaps. We're all crippled and shortsighted in some way, physically or spiritually or mentally." She huffed out a tense breath and slid her gaze to the window.

He thought she'd finished, but she looked back and lowered her voice to a near whisper. "You're more of a complete man than anyone I've ever known." One side of her mouth twitched.

"Besides my dad."

Toby's arrival provided Eli the escape he needed, and he

rerouted his compounding emotions through a stiff cough into his elbow.

"Allergies?" Toby said as he set two burger baskets on the table and a third one heaped with a mix of regular and sweet potato fries.

"No," Eli cleared his throat. "But could I get a glass of water? Two glasses?"

"Sure thing. Enjoy."

Laura's chest rose and fell as she breathed deeply and struggled with her emotions. Good thing Toby had shown up when he did. No telling what she would have said next.

She knew Eli wouldn't pray with her in public. He didn't pray in his own house, but she bowed her head anyway and offered silent thanks for the wounded warrior across from her.

When she looked up she caught him watching her. She'd give her new boots to know what he was thinking.

"Smells like the real deal," she said, her mouth watering at the grilled beef promise. Lifting the top bun, she pushed aside lettuce and tomato and squirted a ketchup circle on the thick ground-meat slab. Then she dotted in two eyes and a smiling mouth.

Eli choked on his bite, laughing.

"What? Don't like the idea of a happy meal?

He held the napkin to his mouth, coughed hard and shook his head. "You make me laugh, Laura Bell."

She shot him a warning look, but he'd already stopped before tacking on the irritating nickname. "Somebody's got to cheer you up."

"You always were full of surprises," he said. "I remember the day you told me you toe-tipped all the way down to the pond."

The words tugged at her heart. "Mom always said toe-tipping was more fun than tiptoeing." She reached for a copper-colored fry and took a bite. Then she took another bite, and another. "Wow, these are good."

"Told you," he said with a serious nod.

"No wonder you're surviving on fried fish at home, if you eat here often enough." She sipped the creamy root beer, smoothed now by the melted ice cream. "But it's not exactly health food."

He grabbed a handful of fries, dropped them in his basket and swirled ketchup over the top. "I'm not much of a lettuce eater."

"Unless it comes on meat with a bun."

He pointed a French fry at her. "You got me there."

The door opened and Laura turned to see several teenagers walk in, followed by a family with two young children. The place was much more crowded than when they arrived. Several people sat on a long bench in front of the window.

"Busy place," she said.

Eli looked over her shoulder and scanned the room, then checked his watch. "Dinnertime. This is not just the best place to eat in town, it's the *only* place this time of day."

They finished their meal, and Eli pulled out his wallet and headed for the cashier. Laura lifted her glass on pretense of finishing the float. "Be right there," she said.

He took the bait and turned away. She slid from the booth and hurried to the picture wall across the room.

Champion 4-H steers, sheep, hogs, rabbits and goats posed with beaming youngsters in traditional county fair photos. Old black-and-white prints highlighted the town's history, and several newspaper clippings boasted the names of graduates, notable locals and deceased old-timers. A few wild rodeo shots brought a smile to her lips, and then she saw it. The framed color portrait of a clean-shaven young man in U.S. Marine blues and white cap. Serious. Proud. In a separate frame below the photo, a newspaper headline shouted what people at her mother's funeral had whispered. Local Man Injured: Lone Survivor of Roadside Attack.

No wonder.

Eli waited in his pickup, the same sober look stamped on

his face as in the picture. He leaned across the seat and pushed her door open.

"Can I say—"

"Don't."

She shot him her most furious glare. "—that was best burger I've ever had."

His jaw clinched. He took his hat off and set it on the box between them and ran both hands through his hair. "Sorry."

Garcia was right. Eli's biggest wound wasn't physical, and right now it gaped open—bold and bloody and untended.

Lord, give me wisdom.

"What happened to Pete's Café?" She refused to add to the injury. They'd had enough trauma for one evening.

Eli must have agreed, for he backed out and onto the street with a more relaxed expression. "It's still up here on the left, next to the real estate office. Just open for breakfast and lunch now."

"Dad used to take us there sometimes for biscuits and gravy." She chuckled. "More health food."

"They still serve it. That's their specialty."

They cruised by the closed café and Laura noticed several empty storefronts. "Looks like the town isn't as prosperous as before."

"The economy has hurt the smaller businesses. Especially in a place as remote as Spring Valley. Not many people other than ranchers come through here, except tourists on their way to the national park in the summer."

"But that's part of the charm, don't you think? Small town and all that. Personally, I've had enough city life to last me forever."

She pulled her hair back and leaned against the door for the full effect. "Smells like alfalfa."

"Hastings recently cut his." He pointed ahead to the right and soon they drove past a green field shaved flat with the cuttings laid out in neat rows. "No doubt he's hoping it'll dry before we get another rain."

Longer shadows reached out from trees and buildings as they headed back, and evening settled around them with a peaceful sigh. As they neared Eli's ranch, a male pheasant dashed across the road, his white-banded neck held aloft. Eli slowed along his fence line, taking in his operation from an outside perspective, then returned his attention to the road as they approached the S-curve.

"Do you mind stopping so I can check for mail?"

"Sure." He turned off at her lane, slowed to a stop and put the truck in park.

"Be right back," she said.

Laura hurried to the bright bell and tugged her box open. Empty. Maybe she should subscribe to the local paper or a magazine.

"Expecting news?" Eli asked when she returned.

"Not really. I guess it's a habit. Most everything I do is on-line. It's just that sometimes I think it would be fun to get a letter, but I don't know who would write to me."

He gave her an odd look as he shifted gears and took the hill.

At the top he parked next to the Mercedes and shut off the engine. In no apparent hurry to leave, he popped his seat belt and relaxed his arm on the open window frame.

"I forget about this view."

"I know. I'm surprised all over again every time I come home. You'd think I'd get used to it."

Considering the beauty before them, she added, "It's really the only thing I found unchanged on my return. Everything else is different."

He scanned the panorama, turning his head as he looked to the right.

"Same thing when I got back from Afghanistan, though I wasn't gone as long as you. Granddad was different, more frail. Garcia was a little more bent and gray. Goldie aged, and of course everything I did required a change on my part."

She glanced sideways at him, wondering if he would talk about what happened.

"But the cattle and the horses and the land were exactly like I remembered them." He looked at her then. "They helped me get my balance."

"What about God?"

Eli sat quietly for so long she thought he hadn't heard her. She didn't want to repeat the question, and decided the timing must not be right.

In a tight, thick voice, his answer broke the silence.

"God didn't help me when I got blown out of the Humvee. I didn't expect His help when I got home, and I don't need His help now."

Tears pushed at her eyes, but she knew he'd think she pitied him. Would he believe her if she told him they were tears of sorrow because he'd missed out on the greatest comfort and help of all?

The sun settled lower and the night sounds stirred. Crickets sang and the bull frog tested his voice. Her resident owl called across the hillside, answered moments later by another.

"How do you know he didn't help you?" she said softly. "You could have died."

"I used to wish I had."

He answered quickly, without pause or consideration. A longtime, deep-seated reply.

Laura removed the box from the seat and scooted closer. She felt him go tense again as she reached across him, laid her hand on his left cheek and turned his head to face her.

"I'm glad you didn't. I'm so very glad you didn't."

Chapter 16

Eli lay on his back, staring through the dark at the ceiling he knew was there but couldn't see.

Laura stirred things he'd long since buried, and he didn't particularly enjoy digging up the remains. He touched his cheek. He didn't know which burned more—the warmth of her fingers or the heat of her words.

She'd invited him to go to church with her tomorrow, and he'd dismissed her invitation with a huff and curtly refused. Why couldn't he at least have been civil about it? She wasn't the enemy.

Was there an enemy?

He'd not considered an identity, but he lived on alert against some unknown assailant. He'd targeted the punk at the feed store, and he focused a lot of his anger on the cattle rustlers.

Maybe *he* was the enemy. His own stubborn attitude and resentment.

He rolled to his side and through his upstairs window had a clear view of Laura's hill. A light glowed from the west end of the house, probably her bedroom. Her porch light cast a thin yellow film that haloed the front door. It blinked.

He stared, waiting for the light to blink again or go out. Maybe Laura had flicked it off and on. Then the light from her room dimmed as something partially blocked it.

Adrenaline shot through his arms and legs. He bolted and grabbed his jeans. Forgetting his leg, he nearly fell when he tried to stand. Frantic he plopped back to the bed, reached for his booted prosthesis and attached it beneath his pant leg.

He grabbed his cell phone, took the stairs two at a time and pulled his other boot on in the back porch. On his way to his truck he called Laura's number. She finally answered as he sped down his road toward the pavement.

"Hi." Her soft voice squeezed his heart and he thought he would choke.

"Laura, I'm on my way up. Don't go to the door. Don't leave your room. Turn off the light."

Silence.

"Laura?"

"Eli, what are you thinking?"

"Are your doors locked?"

"Yes, of course."

"Are you in your bedroom?"

"Eli!"

"Is your room on the west end of the house?"

"What's going on?"

"Turn off the light and get away from the windows. I'll be there in less than a minute."

He ended the call and shoved the accelerator to the floor.

The truck rocked through the S-curve as his headlights jerked right and then left. Skidding into the right turn at Laura's lane, he geared down into second and gunned up the hill. An intruder would hear him coming and probably take off. Better that than getting there too late.

At the top of her hill he stopped in the driveway and killed his lights and engine. From the glove compartment he retrieved a mag light and a 9 mm pistol, then he pulled the keys from the ignition.

Instinctively he crouched, ran to the end of the house and hugged the wall as he eased to the front corner. He stopped. Listened. Waited. A board squeaked. He crossed his wrists, the gun in his right hand, the mag light in his left. Raising them together, he clicked the light as he stepped around the corner and shouted.

"Stop!"

The light caught the prowler's legs as he dived off the porch and ran for the road.

Eli followed him to the head of Laura's drive where he aimed his gun into a corner of the pasture and fired into the dirt. The report echoed through the hills and silenced the crickets.

Satisfied that he'd scared whoever had been snooping around, he stuck his gun in the back of his jeans and returned to the front porch.

He pounded the door. "Laura. It's me. Eli."

In a moment she replied. "Eli?"

"Yes."

"Prove it."

He smiled. "New boots, red tops, burgers and fries."

The lock clicked, the handle turned and in the thin yellow light the door cracked open. Laura reached out, pulled him in and then quickly slammed the door and locked it. The sight of her silky nightshirt and a shotgun in her arms was not an image he'd prepared for.

Suddenly self-conscious, she thrust the gun at him. "Be right back."

He admired the old Winchester and eased the hammer back, grateful that Laura hadn't blown a hole in her front door and him.

She returned in cutoffs and a T-shirt and took the gun. "Thank you. Again."

On tiptoe she stretched and lightly kissed his cheek. "How did you know?"

He glanced at the sofa, surprised she'd have something so worn.

"Oh, please, have a seat. Would you like something to drink? Hot tea? Ginger ale? Water?"

"No thanks." Adrenaline still shot through his veins. "This isn't exactly a social call."

He took the center section of the couch and she sat at his left, holding the gun. Scratches and mews caught his ear and he looked toward the kitchen.

"That's Pete and Re-Pete, my kittens."

"You going to hold that all night?" He nodded at the shotgun.

"Oh." She went to her bedroom, returned empty handed and again sat on his left side. "How did you know?"

Hesitant to admit his sleeplessness and aerial view of her house, he knew only the truth would satisfy her. "I couldn't sleep and I looked out my window and saw your porch light flicker. At first I thought it was going out. Then something passed in front of your bedroom window."

She blanched at his explanation and tucked her feet beneath her. "Did you hit him?"

"No. I shot into the dirt. I just wanted to scare him." He leaned in and laid a hand on hers. "I really don't shoot people. But when they're sneaking around where they shouldn't be, I don't mind scaring them a little."

She shuddered and turned her hand over to link her fingers in his.

It didn't help his adrenaline flow.

"So you were *watching* me?"

"No. Honestly. My window looks out to the north. Your house is in view, but so are all the hills behind you, and Pennington's place. I happened to be looking in the right direction at the right time."

"Do you think it was Pennington?" Her fingers squeezed a little tighter.

"No. Not the way this person moved. Pennington couldn't scramble off the porch like that without breaking his neck. I think it was a kid. In the morning I'll check for footprints. Until then, I want you to come home with me."

For all her trembling, he saw the hackles rise at his insinuation that she couldn't take care of herself. "I do have a shotgun. That piece of iron I was holding when you got here?"

"I understand. I'm not asking for *you*. I'm asking for *me*."

Mentally she weighed his words and he saw it in her eyes.

"I'll never sleep if I think you're in any danger," he said. "And I need to sleep. I've got a fence to build."

She caved at his attempted humor, and her fingers relaxed. "Just tonight."

"Just tonight. We'll figure out something else tomorrow." He reached to adjust his patch and a cold wave of nausea swept through him.

Her hand tightened. "What? What's wrong?"

He tried to disengage his fingers but she wouldn't let go.

"Eli, what's the matter?" Fear returned to her eyes and guilt twisted his gut for causing it.

"Nothing's wrong. I forgot my patch."

Visibly relieved she closed her eyes and expelled a long sigh. When she looked at him again, she searched his face, touching his right eyelid with her gaze and his chest with her free hand.

"*This* is where you are." She pushed slightly against his heart. "The Eli I remember. The Eli I'm so glad to know again."

She stood in her bedroom hugging her arms and uttered a prayer of thanks.

Her ringing phone had been the first jolt. Then Eli's seemingly suggestive remarks. By the time she realized someone crept outside her house, she'd become a quivering mass of jelly holding a loaded shotgun. She fought images of Pennington breaking through her door, but the sound of Eli's gunfire wrenched her stomach. Would she really pull the trigger if faced with an intruder?

If Eli had come right out and told her what was going on, she wouldn't have been so rattled by the time he arrived. Or would she? Did it really matter *how* he told her?

God was watching out for her. The Lord used Eli's one eye to see through the night and observe her danger.

The impropriety of staying in the Hawthorne house paled next to her need for security. She stuffed a few things in a large satchel, grabbed her laptop and followed Eli through the French doors, stopping to make sure they were locked.

In the pickup she fastened her seat belt and stared out the window at her house as they drove away.

At the ranch, a yard light shone over the grounds promising safety within its circle. Eli flipped on the back porch and kitchen lights as they walked through the quiet house, seeming to know the brightness helped dispel her fears. She had never been afraid of the dark. But tonight, the thought of what was *in* the dark had terrified her.

"There are three bedrooms upstairs. Mine is the farthest to the left. Pop's is down the hall to the right, but you'd probably be most comfortable in the one off the landing. It's a spare room with a daybed. Nothing fancy, but you'll be safe."

He jerked his head toward the family room where Goldie watched them sleepily from a braided run in front of the fireplace. "I'll be on the sofa. Won't be the first time it's had an occupant."

She hugged her bag against her chest. "I don't want to force you from your room. I could sleep down here with Goldie."

Compassion softened his features and he fingered an errant strand from her face. "I'll sleep better knowing you're up there out of everyone's view and I'm down here."

It was pointless to argue or feign humility. "Thank you," she whispered. "Again."

At the top of the stairs she looked over her shoulder. He put two fingers to his brow and gave a quick nod.

She smiled, walked into the room ahead and closed the door behind her.

Lying across the quilt-covered daybed, she closed her eyes for a moment.

And then morning peeked in the window.

Laura sat up and scanned the room, clearly remembering her arrival. The bed hugged the west wall and an antique dresser and mirror faced her across the room. An oak chest of drawers anchored the south wall next to the door, and a large, rose-patterned area rug covered most of the hardwood floor. Old and unused in who knew how long, the tiny room still conveyed a homey welcome.

At the thought of home she looked through the curtained window into a stately cottonwood's lush canopy. She could see the grounds below and red pipe fence along the backyard, but the tree blocked any view of her hill. If this had been Eli's room, he wouldn't have known someone lurked outside her window. She shuddered.

She dug through her bag for her cell phone to check the time: 7:30 a.m. Eli and Garcia would be out doing chores. Gathering her things, she turned for the door.

Last night she hadn't thought about an upstairs bathroom. Besides Granddad Hawthorne's old room and Eli's, one other door stood across the hall. It might lead to what she needed, or it could be a closet. Only one way to find out.

To her relief, the dark paneled door opened into a small bathroom with a tiny sink, commode and recently installed corner shower. Perfect. She turned on the water to make sure the plumbing worked, and in five minutes the night's terror slid from her skin and her spirit and spiraled down the drain.

A fresh T-shirt, shorts and sandals completed the transformation.

On her way out she paused at Eli's room and peeked around the opened door. Sure enough, he had a north-facing window. She really wanted to see his view. Should she ask, or dart in, take a look and hurry out? Glancing over her shoulder and listening for movement below, she set her bag down and walked in.

His bed was unmade, as if left in a hurry, and the shirt he'd worn yesterday hung over the footboard. A small wooden box rested on his dresser, and a table against the opposite wall held a prosthetic leg and foot with a tennis shoe attached. A matching tennis shoe sat alone on the floor.

Now *she* was the snoop.

Quickly she moved to the window and looked out on the hills that rippled along the valley's northern edge. Her house perched on the closest one, clearly visible. To the east, rose Pennington's granite monoliths and home.

She dashed back to the hall, grabbed her bag and hurried down the stairs. "Thank you, Jesus," she whispered.

A curtain of frying bacon hung in the kitchen, sugar-cured she guessed by the syrupy hint behind it. She held her hand against the half-full pot in the coffeemaker and smiled at the warmth. Choosing a mug from the cupboard, she added sugar and milk and headed out the back door.

Eyes closed, she stood on the back lawn, welcoming the morning sun against her face and body as it, too, banished the shadows of a frightful night. Cows called to their calves, gate hinges creaked, sprinklers pulsed. Goldie barked. The ranch had fully wakened to the day. A day perfectly formed by the Lord's loving hand.

The Lord's day.

Her eyes flew opened as if the little chapel would appear on the yard before her. She might still have time to make it. If she hurried. She walked past the house and looked to her hill. The shortest route lay across the pasture. She glanced at her sandaled feet.

If she took the road, she faced a nearly two-mile walk, and the last half mile all uphill.

Would Eli give her a ride home?

As if summoned, the golf cart shot out from between the

barn and tractor shed with Eli at the wheel. Goldie barked—
a true backseat driver.

Eli rolled to a stop and laid an arm across the steering wheel.

"Good morning." The patch had returned. "Is that the rest
of my coffee you're drinking?"

She held the mug as if in a toast. "Absolutely."

"Give me twenty minutes and I'll get you home to change
for church." He scanned her bare legs and T-shirt. "Unless you
want to go like that."

Chapter 17

A long night on the couch listening to Goldie snore had given Eli a lot of time to think. And the primary thought was gratitude.

Gratitude that he'd noticed the prowler across two pastures. That in itself was a miracle. Gratitude that Laura was unharmed. That she accepted him as he was, and saw him as *more* than he was. Gratitude that she'd agreed to spend the night under the safety of his watch.

And finally, grudging gratitude that he had lived to feel the warmth of her hand against his chest.

And to whom was he grateful? Certainly not himself.

He kicked off the blanket at five-thirty. Only a few short hours remained to finish chores if he planned to make church by eleven.

He almost changed his mind when he found Laura standing in the yard, gazing across the fields. He'd rather spend the day at home with her. But he knew what she wanted, and what he had earlier realized.

The look on her face when he told her his plan validated his rush to finish the morning's work.

She ran upstairs for her bag and joined him in the pickup. "Give me fifteen minutes," she said, "and I'll be ready."

While Laura changed, he walked the outside perimeter looking for any telltale signs from last night's prowler. The porch deck and lawn showed no sign, but out by the driveway, where the pasture thinned into dirt against the asphalt, he found two running footprints and the place where he'd stopped and fired.

The clearest print was a right foot. A boot, not a tennis shoe. He pressed his own size eleven into the fine dirt next to the print—a good two inches longer than the runner's. Had to be a kid or a slight-built man. Or a woman, and he doubted that. A clear picture of the fat-lipped feed store clerk formed in the dark hole behind his patch.

"Ready."

True to her word, Laura stood outside the French doors shortly after their arrival. A sleeveless turquoise dress deepened her tan, and her hair curled softly at her shoulders. If he ever figured out who had been sneaking around, it would take a whole lot more than his physical strength to keep him from doing damage.

"Find anything?" She climbed into the passenger side as he held the door open.

"Yes."

He circled to the driver's side, admitting to himself that he'd found the woman he wanted to spend the rest of his life with.

Taking his place behind the wheel, he buckled in and backed out. "Two prints next to the asphalt, coming from the pasture where I stopped last night and fired. They're pointing toward the lane, so whoever it was took off either down the road or across it and down the gulley. Not much to go on, but it's a boot print."

He turned his head. Her hands rested on a small leather Bible in her lap and she stared straight ahead.

He focused again on the winding road, and at the bottom, he stopped and looked at her. "You all right?"

"Yes, I'll be fine." A harnessed fear edged her voice. "I just feel uncomfortable, like my privacy has been violated, that I'll always have to look over my shoulder."

You could move in to my place.

The thought nearly escaped his mouth but he clamped his jaw and laid his hand on top of hers. "We're going to figure this out."

She turned her hand into his and gave him a tight smile. "I know."

The last time Eli had been in church he was twenty-two and getting ready to ship out. He still had two eyes, two feet and a grandfather.

The Spring Valley Chapel doors stood open and the parking lot overflowed. A young couple with a toddler walked in ahead of them. Eli removed his cowboy hat as he entered the sanctuary.

He saw what Laura meant about returning. Just like the ranch, the chapel was the same, yet different. A slight pressure pinched the inside of his left elbow as she tucked her hand into his bent arm. He eased into the back row on the right and over enough for Laura to fit beside him.

The songs were new but the feeling was the same. Eli didn't sing, but he watched the words projected on a screen at the front. Laura stood close, singing so quietly that he could feel her voice more than hear it. All those years, and they'd never sat together in church. Yet somehow he'd known she could sing.

During the sermon his mind drifted along with his gaze out the long windows. He thought about his moment of clarity in the predawn stillness. That sense of gratitude returned, spreading through what must be his soul, for it pushed away his demons of resentment and regret. He blinked, focusing on the pastor, reacting to something he'd said—a familiar phrase long silenced by life and circumstances.

"If you are in Christ, you are a new creation. The old has gone, and the new has come."

The young preacher spoke with such energy and conviction, that the words ignited sparks in Eli's chest. New? Could he really be new, with a new start, a new life? New hope?

The remainder of the service blurred as Eli stared at the pew ahead and analyzed the preacher's conditional statement. Was he in Christ? The new-creation promise had a big "if" attached to the front end.

Laura tugged on his arm. "Eli," she whispered. "You ready?"

People stood around them, greeting one another and heading outside. Eli rose and followed Laura into the aisle. A couple of old-timers recognized him and pumped his hand in welcome.

"It's sure good to see you here, son," said an aging rancher Eli remembered from his high school days. "And we appreciate what you did for us over there."

The man's faded eyes watered as he shook Eli's hand in a two-fisted grasp.

"Thank you, sir." The old cowboy's emotion touched Eli deeper than he would have expected.

At the door, the pastor extended a hand toward Laura. "Nice to see you again."

She smiled. "Thank you."

"Laura Bell, if I remember?"

She nodded and turned to Eli. "And this is Eli Hawthorne."

"Hello, Eli. I'm Alex Berger. Glad to have you this morning."

The pastor's cheerful sincerity helped explain the crowded sanctuary. Eli returned his greeting with a nod. "Good to be here. And good sermon."

Eli caught Laura's quick look in his direction but continued out the door, making room for others who pressed in behind them. He had let her see nearly everything about him, but he wasn't quite ready to bare his soul.

* * *

Eli remained unusually silent on the drive home, and the black patch prevented Laura from reading his expression.

Was he simply being polite when he commented on the sermon, or did he mean it? Did something in the message strike a note with him?

It certainly had with her—as if God purposely directed Berger's comments straight into her brain. Old and new. Different and the same. She didn't feel any less anxious about a Peeping Tom on her hill, but she'd found encouragement in his words.

"Want to stay for lunch? Garcia's cooked up a pot of beans."

Eli kept his focus on the road but she detected hopefulness in his tone. And the mention of Garcia's beans set her mouth to watering.

"We can discuss what to do about the prowler."

A deal she couldn't refuse. "Okay."

He smiled and in spite of the patch she could see the warmth.

As they turned off the pavement and onto the ranch lane, she saw a long white trailer parked at the turn to the barn. A slight decrease in speed told her Eli had seen it at the same moment.

"Brand inspector," he said as he parked at the barn. "Looks like he's got calves."

Laura exited the pickup and walked to the stock trailer. Wide-eyed youngsters peered out through the rails.

"Morning." A middle-aged man in a straw cowboy hat shook Eli's hand. "I've got something here you might be interested in."

"Si," Garcia added. "Señor Monfort just arrived. He may have recovered our *becerros.*"

"These three have a distinctive *H* brand that's been run with a rocker," Monfort said. "Looks like a fresh burn to me."

"Where'd you find them?" Eli peered through the slatted trailer, nudging an animal away from the side.

"At a scale in the next county. Authorities there took the truck driver into custody, and notified me after the arrest. The guy had a full semi load, and I'm sorting through the brands. I think these three may be yours."

Eli pointed to the holding pen. "Back up over there and we'll take a look." He headed for the barn and returned with a coiled rope.

Monfort angled the trailer around and into a pen at one end of a long paddock. Garcia opened the trailer door and flushed out the three black calves. They bunched in a corner and started bawling as Eli swung a loop over their heads.

He dropped the loop on the front calf and jerked the slack, holding it taut against his thigh. Garcia walked down the rope, grabbed the animal at the loop and a flank and took it to the ground, holding it down with a knee on its hind quarters.

In the distance a cow called and the little fellow answered.

Eli stooped to inspect the pink flesh showing on the calf's right hip. Through the fence Laura could see a fresh semi-circle burned in an upturned crescent beneath the Hawthorne *H*.

Garcia took the rope off its neck and let the calf up. "This one is ours."

"They're all carrying the same mark," Monfort said.

Eli coiled his rope and motioned for Garcia to join him. Together they crowded the calves and let them run out one at a time. A fresh burn showed on each right hip below the *H*.

Three dry cows watched from the near end of the north pasture, bawling for their calves. "Can they be reunited?" Laura asked.

"We can try." Eli climbed over the fence. "But the cows may be completely dry by now. If they are, we'll stick these babies in with the dairy bunch."

Garcia opened a gate on the opposite side and drove the calves through it. Then he closed the main gate and Monfort pulled the trailer away, stopped and rolled down his window.

Eli approached the truck and tipped his hat back. "I think I know where they're taking them once they pick 'em off."

"Yeah?" Monfort handed Eli a clipboard with paperwork to sign.

"See that draw between those two hills?"

Monfort followed Eli's gesture and studied the low dip. "You think they're driving them through that saddle?"

"The rodeo grounds are directly below it on the other side. It'd be a short trip for a couple of riders to herd them down to the holding pens and then trailer them out."

Monfort nodded slowly and rubbed his chin. "You could be right. You willing to set up a sting?"

Eli's lips curled in a grin that sent chills down Laura's spine. She'd hate to be the rustlers.

"You got that right. We watched one night and discouraged a fella from making off with a calf from the upper pasture. His horse ran off over that draw."

Monfort gave Eli a serious look. "I'm not going to ask what you did because I'm sure it was illegal."

"Don't ask, don't tell," Eli said with no humor in his cold tone.

"Let me know when, and I'll have someone camped out under cover. You two follow at a distance and maybe we can catch them in the act."

"There's no moon tomorrow night. That too soon for you?"

Monfort shook his head, set the clipboard beside him in the seat and put his truck in gear. "I'll have somebody over there before dark." He nodded and eased down the dirt lane toward the pavement raising a wake of low dust behind him.

The cows had moved down the fence until they stood directly across from the penned babies. Garcia opened a back gate and the little blacks loped across the lane. Buckling their front knees, all three inched under the pipe fence and headed for lunch.

Laura watched, enthralled by the homecoming. The scene tugged at her overworked emotions and her eyes teared. Eli walked up beside her and put an arm around her shoulders with a quick squeeze. "Quite a sight, isn't it?"

She nodded, afraid that if she opened her mouth her voice wouldn't work.

Chapter 18

The aroma of simmering beans with onion and green chili nearly knocked Laura over when they entered the back porch. Her stomach rallied with a loud snarl.

"Pete and Re-Pete," she said with a gasp. "I forgot to let them out."

Eli washed his hands in the sink and dried them as he answered. "They'll be fine. I'll take you home after lunch and you can let them out."

Guilt pushed her to insist they go immediately, but Eli wasn't a taxi service. And he was right—another hour wouldn't starve them. She'd left a full bowl the previous evening before the prowler incident, and they never cleaned out their dish overnight.

"Mija," Garcia began. "Can you make corn bread for our beans?"

Happy to be useful, she patted the man's shoulder and took a large bowl from the cupboard. "I sure can. Glad you asked."

Eli busied himself at the opposite counter with a long knife and a longer watermelon. He quickly chopped the melon in half, sliced green-rimmed circles of deep pink, then cut them into quarters and placed them on a serving platter.

Thirty minutes later—with fresh corn bread on the table— they all took a seat.

Laura bowed her head as always, but this time Eli reached for her hand.

"Thank You, Lord, for this meal and for protecting Laura last night. And thank You for bringing some of our stock home."

His mention of her name tied a knot in her throat and kept her head down and her eyes closed, but Garcia offered a quiet *"Gracias, amén."* Something had indeed happened inside Eli since their last meal together.

Cutting the hot, yellow bread into squares, she served the men and then buttered her own thick slice. Garcia's flavorful beans filled their bowls, their quiet mouths and finally their grateful stomachs.

"I can never get mine to taste as good as yours, *abuelito*," Laura said.

His dark eyes shone with a secret pride. "Keep trying, *mija*. Someday you will get them just right."

Setting his bowl aside, Eli reached for a watermelon slice. "You've got two options regarding the prowler," he said, slicing his fork through the watery fruit.

Immediately sobered, she fixed him with an intent look. "And they are?"

"A motion sensor light with an alarm, or a big dog."

She let out a heavy sigh.

"Motion sensors are inexpensive," he continued, "and immediate, but visiting critters might set them off."

"Visiting critters?" She thought of Pennington.

"Skunks, raccoons. It might be interesting to sprinkle flour on your porch some evening to see what tracks are left by morning."

"That's amazing," she said, truly intrigued. "I've never thought of such a thing."

He reached for another melon slice. "Dogs cost more, plus you have the ongoing expense of feeding one, not to mention the time it takes for one to mature. Unless you buy a full-grown dog to begin with."

"But I've read that dogs are the number one deterrent to home burglars."

"Unless they are our Goldie." Garcia grinned.

Eli chuckled and forked the last pink bite from the rind. "And they're better company than a light and alarm."

Laura knew how much he loved the old retriever. It wouldn't be long, and he might be looking for another companion.

A related thought fluttered through her mind, one she quickly swallowed with corn bread and butter.

With assaults on two fronts—a snoop at Laura's and cattle thieves at his place—Eli considered his options. He'd prefer to have Laura stay at the ranch, but she refused for obvious reasons. Even Garcia had raised his ragged brows when Eli suggested it at lunch.

He could camp out on her hill in the dark and leave Garcia below to watch the ranch, but that spread their defenses too thin. Laura's decision made the most sense. She would get a dog *and* motion detectors that she could turn off during the day. The double coverage would help restore her sense of privacy and provide safety.

She also had the shotgun, but he didn't know if she could use it if someone broke in on her.

Honestly, he hoped he never learned the answer to that question.

Sunday afternoon he and Garcia saddled up and drove the reunited cow-calf pairs from the north pasture into the neighboring section which happened to be the farthest to the east. The one they hoped the thieves would target Monday night.

He and Garcia would be waiting in the apple orchard with

night vision goggles and mounts ready. Things might get real Western by the time they boxed the rustlers in against the brand inspector's men at the rodeo grounds.

Monday's five forty-five alarm sounded as Laura lay wide awake listening to the faint rumble of Eli's tractor engine in her lower pasture. She punched the button and dived back into bed, grateful for a quiet night, but not quite ready to leave her nest. She'd driven into town Sunday afternoon and purchased two motion detector lights. The hardware-store clerk tested the alarms for her, and she firmly believed their ungodly racket would either chase off any would-be intruder or frighten him to death.

She'd easily installed them herself, one on the front porch and one on the back. And since she'd slept through the night unawakened by the raucous clamor, she evidently hadn't had any "visiting critters," either.

She smiled to herself at Eli's comment about skunks and raccoons.

So much for happy memories—or unsettling ones. Mary would be at their rendezvous point by six sharp, and the kittens sounded like two elephants tumbling in the laundry room. Time to get up.

Laura drove down the hill, feeling less vulnerable with a vehicle. She might need a little time to shake the sensation of being watched. Even in the daytime.

Proud to be at the edge of the road when Mary came into view, she was surprised to see another runner—a girl about eight or nine years old. She must be Mary's bread-baking granddaughter.

"Good morning," Mary said. She laid a hand on the child's shoulder. "Lily, this is Laura Bell, the friend I told you about."

"Nice to meet you." The little red-haired girl held her hand out with a grown-up expression in her green eyes.

"And it's nice to meet you, too," Laura said with a smile. "What grade will you be in next fall?"

"Fourth."

"Well, I might see you sometime if I get to be a substitute teacher for your school."

"Lily here is quite the little homemaker," Mary said. "She's the one who bakes snicker doodle bread for me and her grandpa."

The girl raised her chin with an air of self-confidence.

"We'll have to compare recipes, Lily. After I saw your grandmother eating your bread one morning in her store, I came right home and tried baking a loaf myself."

"Did you eat it all?"

"No, I gave some to a friend."

"Grandma?"

Laura felt a blush slide across her cheeks. "No, to my neighbor who lives on the ranch below. We'll go right by his pastures on our run."

"Speaking of which, we'd better get going if I'm going to stay on schedule." Mary flexed her legs and set off down the road.

Lily easily kept up with her grandmother, and Laura's pride took a not-so-subtle hit. She was about to be outrun by generations on each end of her personal timeline.

She wanted to mention the peeping Tom, but not in Lily's hearing. On their return, she held back and managed to catch Mary's attention. The woman slowed her pace and Lily continued on ahead.

"Thanks for slowing," Laura said.

"Are you still sore?"

"No, I just want to tell you about something that happened, but I don't want to frighten Lily."

Mary frowned and scrutinized Laura's face. "Is everything all right?"

"Not exactly. Someone was prowling around outside my place Saturday night. Apparently looking in my windows. I installed motion sensors with alarms yesterday afternoon. They weren't set off last night, so that's good news."

Mary slowed to a walk and looked ahead at her granddaughter who had stopped near Laura's road. "How do you know someone was there? Did you hear them?"

Suddenly Laura felt uneasy about explaining Eli's discovery of the prowler, but Mary didn't seem to think it odd.

"Thanks for letting me know. I'll tell Rich and a few other people to be on the lookout."

"Eli thinks it may be a teenager," Laura said. "Are there any young men living up the road that you know of?"

"Oh, I'm sure there are. I'll check around and get back to you."

They parted at the mailboxes and as Mary and Lily continued on, Laura momentarily considered the bright yellow bell on the third box from the right end. Then she turned away and walked to her car, clicked the key lock and slipped inside.

On the way to the house she wondered how Pete and Re-Pete would feel about a canine roommate.

The animal shelter employee remembered Laura from her earlier visit.

"How are the kittens?" she asked as they walked back to the dog kennels.

"Growing like the national debt," Laura said. "They are more fun than I could have imagined."

"Yeah, they were a playful pair." She walked past two rows and turned into an aisle that echoed with howls and barks and whimpers.

Laura began to doubt whether she could get out of the shelter with just one animal.

"What exactly are you looking for?" the employee asked.

"I need a watchdog. But I don't want one that's going to bite friendlies. And I don't know if I want a full-grown dog or one that I can raise myself."

The caretaker stopped before a concrete-block and chain-link enclose. A sad-eyed pit bull lay on its belly, head on paws.

Laura knew the breed had gotten a bad rap, but she wasn't

ready for a full-grown, unknown entity with a grisly reputation. "Maybe not," she said softly.

The next kennel harbored two baying black-and-tan hound puppies that were all leg and ear and tail. And voice. Laura covered her ears and shook her head. "Sorry."

Cage after cage held everything from adorable lap dogs to pitiful abandonment cases. This was not working out so well. Maybe she needed to do a little research before making a commitment.

And then she saw the little blue heeler pup sitting quietly on its haunches, pointed ears up, eyes alert.

"What about him?" she asked.

"You mean *her.*"

The caretaker opened the gate and knelt before the puppy that licked her extended hand and attempted to wag its stubby tail. "This one's a keeper, I tell you. If someone doesn't take her, I'm going to talk my husband into it." She looked up with a guilty expression. "That's the downside of working here. I keep taking home the orphans."

Laura could name a few other downsides, but kept the more depressing thoughts to herself. She held out a hand and the puppy showered her with kisses, as well.

"Does she have a name?"

"Not yet." The woman stood and pulled the gate closed, and moved on to the next kennel. The puppy yipped once, and Laura took a step back and peeked around the wall. It sat with its head cocked to one side, those sharp black ears pointed skyward. Intelligent eyes bore into hers and seemed to promise protection and companionship.

"I'll take her."

Laura left the puppy at the shelter, and drove into town for a dog carrier, a new collar and chain, puppy food, a bed and doggy treats. After the challenges of getting the kittens home in a cardboard box on her floorboard, the carrier was a must.

But rather than whimper and fight its confinement, the little heeler lay quietly, head on paws, watching Laura through the carrier's metal-grate door.

"What's your name?" Laura asked. Each time she spoke, the dog perked its ears.

"You don't strike me as a house dog, but I can't let you run all over the hills."

She slowed and turned left onto the county road. "We have coyotes."

At that, the pup raised its head and gave a little yip.

"Don't worry, I'll let you sleep inside until you're all grown up. Or build a kennel for you. Would you like that?"

Dark chocolate eyes watched her from atop gray mottled paws.

At her turn, Laura slowed and her eyes were drawn to the yellow bell. Rather than adding to her good memories, it taunted her, as if ringing out, "No mail—no mail again today."

She might have to remove it.

Laura took the carrier to the front porch, then returned to the car for her purchases. She set the dog food bag against one French door and unlocked the other.

"Welcome home," she said as she brought the carrier inside.

Curious mews from the laundry room greeted her, and when she opened the door, the kittens darted out like rockets. Until they saw the dog.

Arching their spines like Halloween cats, they flattened their ears and flared their tails and stalked sideways in front of the puppy.

"Be nice, you guys. This is your new roommate."

Laura sat cross-legged next to the carrier, pinched the lock open and reached in, pulling the little heeler into her lap. Pete and Re-Pete hissed and posed, and she laughed at their posturing.

"So, boys, what do we call our new little lady?"

Chapter 19

Eli set and tamped the last post several yards east and down-hill from Laura's house. She'd driven in about thirty minutes earlier, and the thought of ice-cold water and her sweet smile seemed mighty good at the moment. He took his hat off and waved it at Garcia who lifted his welder's mask.

Eli jerked his head toward the house. "Let's go up for some water."

Garcia set the helmet aside, grabbed his hat and secured his equipment.

On the shaded front porch, Eli slapped his hat against his dusty jeans, sleeved the sweat from his face and knocked. Circumstances had been a lot different when he'd knocked two nights ago. He noted the motion sensor above the doorframe.

This time Laura swung the door wide and stood holding a blue heeler pup that gurgled a throaty growl.

"These are the friendlies, girl. No growling." She stroked the little dog's head and stepped back for the men to enter.

"We're dirty," Eli said. "We'll just borrow your shade out

here. But we could sure use some ice water." He eyed the pup. "Nice dog."

"Thank you. And absolutely." She came outside. "You've got the swing there, and I'll bring another chair. Guess I need furniture out here, don't I?"

Garcia murmured softly and offered the back of his hand to the puppy. *"Ah, chica bonita,"* he crooned. "She will be a good dog for you."

The puppy lowered her ears and licked his hand.

"She likes you, and you may have solved my problem." Laura buried her face against the dog's neck. "How about Chica? Would you like that?"

The puppy squirmed and licked her face.

"Would you hold her for me while I get you men something cold to drink?" She offered the wiggly bundle to Eli who scooped the pup into his arms and took a seat on the steps.

Garcia claimed the swing and fanned himself with his palm leaf hat.

Laura returned with a chair, but took her time with the water. Eli considered looking for a hose when the screen door opened and she stepped through with a tray of sandwiches and two glasses of ice water.

"You don't have to feed us," Eli said, getting to his feet.

"Yes, I do. It's lunch time." She held the tray for Garcia who helped himself to a glass and two sandwiches.

"Gracias, mija," he said.

She set the tray on the porch railing, and Chica squirmed from Eli's arms into hers.

"She hasn't moved this much all morning," Laura said. "You seem to have brightened her day."

Eli propped his hat on the railing, picked up a sandwich and glass, and took a long, cold drink. Then he joined Laura on the steps. "We're about finished with the fence," he said between bites. "I'll be pulling cable and Garcia's got a few more pipes to weld. Then we'll pull out the old T-posts and barbed wire."

The dog finally wiggled from Laura's hold and bounded

across the porch to Garcia. A worried look bunched Laura's brows.

Eli reached for her hand. "She'll be okay. Let her sniff around, get to know her territory."

"You're probably right," she said, and leaned against his arm. "The fence—you were talking about the fence." She straightened and looked toward the lower pasture. "It great. What a relief to not have to worry about Pennington's stock pushing through."

"Speaking of cattle, how's your herd?"

She gave him a scalding look. "You're mocking me."

"Not even a little." He reined in the laughter that pawed in his chest. "You've got five head—that makes a herd. And now you've got a cow dog."

"And boots, don't forget," she said.

"You're all set. All you need is a horse."

A mew through the screen door turned their heads.

"How are the kittens taking to the pup?"

"I think they're offended."

He laughed and pushed himself up. "I see you got your motion sensor installed. Glad it didn't go off this morning when we walked up here."

Laura stood and took his empty glass. "Boy, are you ever. It makes an ungodly racket."

"That's the whole idea." He put his hat on and thought about kissing her.

"You have chosen a fine dog." Garcia crossed the porch and gave his glass to Laura.

The puppy bounded down the steps and sniffed its way across the yard and into the bushes.

"I hope so. I want her to be a good watchdog, but friendly, too. That might be too much to expect."

"No worry, *mija*." Garcia smiled broadly and dipped his wide hat with a nod. "Thank you for the cold water." He patted his stomach. "And for filling our empty bellies. Now we will finish."

Garcia walked down the steps and eased through the barbed wire. Laura watched the puppy exploring the yard, and Eli slipped his arm around her waist, hoping he hadn't misread her over the past few days. She turned into him and swept his face with her beautiful eyes.

"May I kiss you?" he whispered.

Her lips curved in a perfect smile and she closed her eyes with a "Yes."

Laura watched the two cowboys hike down the hillside toward the fence line. She hugged her arms and relived the moment Eli's warm lips touched hers, but a yip drew her attention to the bushes. Pulling away from the tingling memory, she trotted down the steps to investigate.

"Chica—come, Chica." The puppy backed out of the bougainvillea that had overgrown one end of the house and bounded to her. "Good girl." She sat on the grass and rubbed the dog's upturned belly as it wiggled its back against the scratchy grass. "You're more playful than I expected. But don't forget you have a job to do."

The pup rolled to its feet and gave her chin a fullhearted washing. Laughing, Laura carried it indoors.

She set Chica on the floor, went to the sofa and her laptop and settled in with an eye on the kittens. Pete and Re-Pete would have to make their own peace with the newcomer.

Checking her email disheartened her almost as much as checking her mailbox, except it wasn't completely empty. Junk and a few bills. She closed the site and began a search for dog runs, starting with "images" to get a few ideas.

They were as varied as the animals themselves. Large, small, wooden, chain link, covered, uncovered. She didn't want a cage, but she didn't want to fence in the entire hilltop either. The local hardware store's website didn't offer much, but a wider search of the Spring Valley area brought up the feed store.

Apprehension wormed in as she clicked on the link for livestock fencing. A dog and two cats weren't exactly livestock, but she had to start somewhere.

Of course they had exactly what she wanted.

A loud hiss drew her attention to the kitchen. Chica had the kittens cornered against one wall and the French doors. They swiped at her with their little paws and hissed. She hunkered down with her rear in the air and darted forward with a snap of her jaws.

"Play nice."

At the sound of Laura's voice, Chica turned, the kittens dashed away and the chase was on.

Laura looked again at the feed store page and rolled her lips. She couldn't do it, wouldn't do it. She wouldn't ask Eli to take her back there and she wouldn't have them deliver the materials. What if the tobacco-chewing clerk was the delivery boy?

She logged off.

The chain she'd bought reached far enough to give Chica room to poke around until she could get a kennel. She simply needed a good place to attach it.

That evening Laura shut the kittens in the laundry room with fresh food and water, and took Chica outside. She attached the long chain to the dog's collar and clipped the opposite end around the mulberry tree.

"Go potty," she told the puppy as it wagged its whole rear end trying to wag its stubby tail.

Laura relaxed in the swing and gave it a little shove. A distant coyote called and she checked for Chica's reaction. The pup sat on its haunches and aimed its ears across the valley toward the hills. A little growl rumbled in its chest.

Good dog.

She pushed the swing again and surveyed the ranch below. The sprinklers were silent and a light in the ranch house told her the men were in the kitchen. Probably having dinner and planning for tonight.

Tonight. The thought chilled her and she rubbed her arms. Eli and Garcia planned to lay in wait for rustlers, and if they came, follow them over the draw to the rodeo grounds. Hopefully the brand inspector hadn't forgotten. What if Eli got there and had no backup?

"Lord, please watch over my boys tonight." The endearing term warmed the once-empty place in her core, and her eyes locked on the end of the new fence where the old tree stood. Could her heart be mending?

Pan-fried burgers and beans waited on the table in Eli's kitchen, but only two plates. He wanted to make it three, but he didn't want to spook Laura. She'd just come out of a painful relationship. In spite of her warm response to his kiss, he didn't want to spoil things by rushing her.

He took a seat and passed the beans to Garcia who bowed his head. Embarrassed that he'd forgotten, Eli set the bowl down and lowered his eyes.

"*Gracias, Señor,* for this food and this land. Protect us and our cattle tonight. *Amén.*"

"Amen."

Eli dumped beans over his meat and ate it with a fork. Garcia doused his meat and beans with green chili and did the same.

"We'll ride out after dark and wait in the orchard near the east section."

Garcia nodded. "Will the inspector's men be waiting at the *rodéo?*"

"I sure hope so." Eli scraped up a bite of beans. "I'd like to put a stop to this whole thing and get on with making a living."

Garcia considered him a moment. "Get on with making a life?"

Eli met his gaze. The old man was doing it again—reading his mind. "That, too."

"She will join you." Garcia took a long drink of iced tea.

"You know this how?"

"I know in here," he said, tapping his chest with a leathery finger. His obsidian eyes sparkled.

Eli's heart tumbled with mixed emotions—a yearning for Laura and a lust for vengeance. They didn't sit well together.

"First things first," he said scraping his chair back. "Let's get this over with."

Eli locked Goldie in the tack room, and like two shadowy trail riders, he and Garcia rode out from the barn. A scabbard at his thigh held the Remington .223. The night vision monocular dangled from a lanyard around his neck, and his cell phone snugged his shirt pocket, locked and silenced, tight against the envelope with Laura's name on the front.

A crazy idea had sent him upstairs for it after dinner.

Garcia's mount was as black as the night. Thermal imaging goggles hung from the saddle horn, and a tightly coiled rope lay over the horn and one swell. The palm leaf rode low on the man's brow, and Eli could easily imagine a full *bandoleer* across his partner's chest.

He was glad Garcia was on his side.

Their slow, choppy steps followed the dirt road until they reached the orchard's softer soil. Riding between the trees, clear of the branches, the two men moved silently into the grove and reined in two rows from the eastern edge.

A distant growl rolled over the hills, and a faint glow flashed in the high country.

"Lightning," Garcia said.

"I hope the storm holds off long enough for those scoundrels to get here."

Eli stepped off his horse and dropped the reins. Lifting his night vision monocular, he scoped the draw above the ranch. "Come on boys. Come and get your prize."

Lightning bounced across the higher ridges and thunder rumbled faintly in the distance, but no one rode over the low place between two hills.

Time itself slept as Eli tracked the lightning strikes, trying to guess the storm's path. He sat against an apple tree and pulled out the note. Unable to read it in the starlight, he fingered the flap and mulled over the idea that had sent him upstairs.

How would she respond if she read it now? Would she think he was mocking her and her wish for a letter? Was he too old to give a child's note to a woman—especially after that kiss? He slid the envelope behind his phone.

Antsy after the long wait, Eli climbed into the saddle and rode forward to see if the cattle were restless. They predicted a coming storm better than any weatherman.

The cows lay still, babies at their sides. A storm wouldn't be here anytime soon unless the wind shifted. Riding back to where Garcia sat like a mounted statue, Eli stopped beside him and pushed the button on his watch: 23:59—nearly midnight.

"Maybe I scared them off for good." The trees muffled his voice and disappointment took hold on his heart. He wanted to catch those greedy thieves red-handed.

Recalling their last stakeout and Laura's sweet bread, he wished he'd packed a loaf. He could use a slice or two right about now.

Garcia shifted in his saddle and the leather squeaked. He pushed his hat off, let it hang down his back on the stampede string and held the goggles to his eyes. "South," he said.

Eli scanned to the right and saw movement. The darkness glowed green through his monocular as two riders loped confidently toward the section fence.

The palms of his hands began to itch and his heart rate increased. He breathed slowly through tight lips and willed himself to remain calm. This wasn't Afghanistan.

The riders paralleled the fence line and stopped at the bottom of the pasture. They dismounted, and one handed his reins to the other and slipped through the fence. He ran to the nearest calf, jerked a piggin' string from his belt and hog-tied the animal. Then he dragged the calf back to the fence where the waiting man yanked it underneath.

The runner repeated his ploy and dragged off another calf. By that time, both mamas were up and calling, answered by their trussed calves. The man slipped through the fence, released the calves and, with his partner, cut them away from the fence and started toward the draw.

The whole thing took fewer than five minutes.

"When they reach the top of the saddle, we'll head out," Eli said.

Garcia returned his palm leaf to his head and tugged the brim down.

They edged from the orchard as the riders crested the draw. Taking the lead down an alleyway between two sections, Eli eased Buddy into a trot. When they reached the open hillside, he and Garcia heeled their horses' sides and loped up the gentle rise. At the top, they reined in, and Garcia pushed his hat back and scanned the slope that rose on either side. Eli scoped the rodeo grounds.

"There they are," he said, pointing toward the holding pens on the arena's north side.

"And a trailer," Garcia added.

"Time for a phone call." Eli hoped the brand inspector's men were waiting, and he hoped they had their phones silenced. He'd hate to get this far and have the whole thing crash on a ring tone echoing through the dark.

"Granger," a quiet voice said.

"You Monfort's man?"

"You Eli Hawthorne?"

"We're up on the saddle west of the rodeo grounds. Following two rustlers with two calves. You should have a couple of visitors in the holding pens on the north side."

"I see 'em. Thanks." The call ended.

An anticlimactic letdown settled in Eli's gut as he headed Buddy down the draw. Garcia rode beside him, as dark and silent as Eli's mood.

A steel trailer door moaned near the pens. And in perfect timing three sets of headlights glared to life, a triangular stranglehold on two panicky cowboys with a couple of wide-eyed calves.

Eli touched his spurs to Buddy's side and hurried to the flat.

Monfort and two others exited the vehicles parked strategically around the holding pens. One was a sheriff's car.

"Put your hands on your head," the deputy hollered, his gun drawn. "Party's over."

In the unforgiving glare, Eli thought one of the two rustlers looked familiar. He took Buddy in for a closer look, and stopped near the deputy as he cuffed the tobacco-chewing clerk from the feed store.

The clerk scowled and spit in Eli's direction. An old reflex jerked Eli's right bicep, but he laid his forearms across his saddle horn and leaned in. "Heck of a way to make a living," he said. Shaking his head, he reined away and walked over to Monfort.

"The skinny one works at the feed store. I don't know the other fella."

"I do," Monfort said. "I suspected his involvement. Works for another rancher about twenty miles from here. His calves have been disappearing, too. Bet I know why."

"Good work tonight," Eli said.

"It wouldn't have happened without your tip about the rodeo grounds. These two aren't the only team stealing stock in the area, I'm sure, but at least they're two more out of commission."

Garcia waited next to the pen where the babies bawled.

"You want to drive them back tonight?" Monfort asked Eli.

"No, but I don't want to leave them here, either. If you don't mind, can I borrow this truck and trailer before you confiscate it?"

"Check with the sheriff. Fine with me if he doesn't mind."

Chapter 20

He minded.

"Sorry, can't do it. It's evidence. And I'm sure the owner wouldn't want to be involved. I ran the plates on the truck and trailer, and they came back belonging to someone other than these two." He jerked a thumb over his shoulder.

"No problem. I understand." Eli turned away and Garcia rode up beside him.

"I will go back and get the stock trailer. Then we will all ride home."

"Sounds good." Eli pushed his hat up. "Thank you, my friend."

Garcia touched his wide brim and loped off toward the hills.

Eli dismounted and threw Buddy's reins across the top rail of the calf pen. Within thirty minutes, another sheriff's car arrived with a driver for the truck, and Monfort, his man and the deputies all pulled out.

Suddenly alone in the dark, Eli slid to the ground and leaned against the holding pen. The moonless night settled around him and he smelled the storm. A bright flash to the east lit the hills in a strobelike scene. It wouldn't be long.

He pulled his hat off and ran his hand through his hair. He thought back to those long, cold nights in the Afghanistan mountains. A man's mind could play tricks on him, make him think someone was out there, when in truth, there were *many* someones out there.

If you are in Christ, you are a new creation.

The pastor's comments from Sunday came to mind, his promise of a new beginning and old things sloughing off. The promise wasn't the pastor's, but God's. The God Eli had known before the explosion.

If you are in Christ, you are a new creation.

The words settled in his chest, beating like some living, breathing thing. Like a heart.

"I want to start over, Lord," he whispered. "But I need a hand here."

Tears pricked his eye and a searing pain cut through the right side of his face. The left foot that he no longer had throbbed with every heartbeat, and he feared he would cry out in agony.

And then it was gone. The pain vanished instantly, and peace bloomed inside his chest like a silent, surreal grenade.

Eli's breath came in short, ragged gasps and he tipped his head back against the rails and stared into the black sky.

The explosion shot Laura straight up from a dead sleep. The house shuddered. Chica yelped and dived under the bed.

Laura's heart pounded in her throat. She pulled on her jeans and a shirt and lifted the dust ruffle. Chica lay trembling, ears down, eyes wide, a small whimper in her throat.

"Come here, girl." She reached for the dog but it scooted back, terrified.

Another crash and blue light cut through the house.

"That was close," she said as she tugged on her tennis shoes. "No pause between the strike and the thunder."

The hair on her arms tingled with electricity. She glanced at the clock on the floor: 3:00 a.m. The red digits winked and then disappeared.

The refrigerator's background hum stopped.

"Great. No power."

The house rattled with another boom and light flashed through the windows. She stood and walked into the living room, staring into the darkness. A blue arrow struck the pasture.

Momentarily blinded, she fell to her knees at the thunder crack, certain the strike had split her house apart as well as her eardrums.

"Lord, protect us. Send Your angels," she prayed. "Or if these massive lightning bolts *are* Your angels, calm them down a bit, please."

Another slash of light and she flinched. This time a second passed before the thunder clap. She squeezed her eyes tight, and another bolt hit with blinding intensity. Two seconds before the resounding boom. The storm was moving.

Laura went to the kitchen, opened the doggy treats she'd left on the counter and returned to her room, determined to extricate Chica.

"Come on Chica *bonita*." She held the tidbit close to the puppy. "Want a treat?"

Whimpering and quaking, the dog raised its ears and stuck its nose forward.

"Come on, honey. It's okay. God's just rearranging his furniture."

Surprised by her childish explanation, her eyes misted. Mama always said that during the most frightening thunderstorms.

A wet nose touched Laura's fingers and she pulled her hand back. "A little more, come on, baby."

The room lit up momentarily but the accompanying rumble sounded farther away.

"The worst is over, Chica. Come and get your treat."

The puppy inched forward, one gray paw at a time, until Laura could finger the collar and pull her out. Chica gobbled the treat and licked Laura's hand looking for more.

Cradling the trembling dog, she went to the kitchen and rewarded the pup with two more bites. Then she opened the laundry-room door hoping the kittens would offer a distraction. She heard them mewing from behind the dryer.

"You big scaredy cats." Chica wiggled from her arms and proceeded to chow down. The sounds of a canine inhaling their food brought the kittens out of hiding, and the games began.

Relieved, Laura retreated to the sofa where she curled up and watched the storm dance across the valley on its way to other counties.

"Thank You, Lord." Relaxing, she nestled against the arm rest and closed her eyes.

A high-pitched yap woke Laura with a start. The automatic ice maker dumped a load of cubes and her alarm clock beeped. Daylight streamed through the windows with no hint of last night's storm. No water dripped from the porch roof. Dry lightning.

Chica yipped again and did what Laura feared might be a potty dance. She rushed to open the front door and the puppy darted out before she remembered the motion sensor.

A deafening wail erupted above her head and she reached to flip the switch.

After checking the time on her laptop, she reset the alarm clock, vowing again to find a nightstand and dresser. Today might be a good day to check out those antique stores she passed the other day with Eli.

A tingling in her belly sat up and took notice.

How gallant he'd been in light of that employee's crude remarks.

Now there was an outdated word—*gallant*—one she might introduce to school children next fall if she got the chance to talk about heroes. She followed that line of thought, imagining

Eli on a white horse, rescuing a threatened damsel—herself, of course.

Derek had never once taken a protective attitude. She shook her head and focused instead on the morning.

Mary had already run and driven to work by now, but it wasn't so late that Laura couldn't run by herself. Apprehension tickled the back of her neck and she pushed it away. She couldn't live her life in fear—or wait for someone else to rescue her. Besides, it was daytime. And she had the car.

Happy with her decision to stick to her exercise schedule, Laura realized this could be a good test for Chica and the chain. She took the puppy's food and water outside and set it beneath the tree. Then she clipped the chain to Chica's collar and gave her ears a good rubbing.

"You be good, okay? I won't be gone long."

The puppy sat and yipped once.

Laura paused at the front door, and a quick glance revealed Chica stretched out on her belly like a frog in the shade.

Smoke pricked Laura's nose. She spent a long moment scanning the valley and hills but saw no tendrils rising and went inside.

After locking both doors, she drove down to the main road, keyed her lock and pocketed the remote. The yellow bell glowed from the mailboxes, bright and bold in the morning sun. So much for happy memories. The thing taunted her.

She hit the pavement and eased into a run, hugging the road's edge through the S-curve and down to the flat. Eli's ranch sprawled at her left, and the ever-singing sprinklers arched across green pastures that contrasted more and more with the drying hills. She ran on, reveling in the beauty and considering what she did *not* see. Traffic. Crowds. High-rise apartments and business offices.

Cattle and trees and barns populated her world. An occasional house, stock trailers and horses. And Eli.

At the entrance to the ranch she slowed, hesitated, wanting to see him again, hear his voice, feel his breath against her cheek. In a few short weeks her childhood friend had become so much more. And if he'd truly turned his heart toward God…

She spun around and ran back toward her car.

At the entrance to the S-curve, she heard an engine revving toward the crest from the other side. Sensing danger, she stepped off the pavement next to a sharp drop-off as Pennington blew by in his pickup. He clearly took his half out of the middle.

What if Mary and Lily had been with her? Anger rumbled in her chest, crowding out her more pleasant thoughts.

Walking now, she cleared the curve. The mailbox row stood at attention, one in particular shouting her name. Enough.

She clicked her remote and searched the glove box for the old screw driver. Looking both ways before she crossed the road, she strode toward the yellow bell with purpose.

She jerked it open and gasped. A faded square envelope lay inside with no postage. No address. Only her name inked in bold block letters: LAURA BELL. A shiver rippled through her as she slid it out.

Indecision and regret hadn't figured much in Eli's life, but now they wrestled for first place.

He and Garcia had unloaded the calves and turned the horses out just ahead of the storm. Then Eli unhooked the trailer and drove to the mailboxes. The first lightning strike lit the road like a spotlight. He tugged on the yellow bell, laid the letter inside and drove back to the ranch before the second-guessing began.

It hadn't taken long.

With every lightning strike he thought of a dozen reasons he shouldn't have left the letter and half as many things that could go wrong because he had. Between the storm outside and the one raging in his head, the night had been short and sleepless.

And hiding his turmoil from Garcia wouldn't be easy either.

Standing in the barn's shade, the old *vaquero* fanned five horseshoe nails between his teeth and tucked Buddy's right front hoof between his knees. He held a sixth nail in his left hand and a small hammer and horseshoe in his right. Positioning the shoe, he deftly drove the nail through the shoe and out the front edge of the hoof, then twisted off the exposed end with the hammer claw.

The next five nails went in the same way. Garcia clenched off the exposed ends and smoothed the rough edges with a rasp. He dropped the foot, straightened and looked Eli in the eye. Then he started the process all over again.

Eli didn't know who was being nailed. His horse or himself.

He held Buddy's lead rope and listened to the tap-and-snip rhythm of the farrier's skill. He'd never learned the trade—probably a mistake as a rancher. But he hadn't seen the need with Garcia around. The man could set four shoes on a good horse in under an hour. A broncy one took a little longer.

"You have changed," Garcia said from beneath his broad brim.

Eli squirmed. "How?"

The older man straightened and stretched his back. "Your eyes are filled with doubt."

"Don't you mean 'eye'?"

Garcia grinned as he slid five more nails between his perfect teeth and stooped to the next hoof.

As a boy, Eli had pulled a few fast ones on his grandfather, but nothing ever got past Garcia. No matter. Eli didn't plan on telling him about the note he'd written twelve years ago and delivered last night.

At least not yet.

Garcia rasped the final hoof smooth, straightened and looked toward Pennington's place.

Eli followed his stare and saw the thin cloud that hung beyond the first rise. A lightning strike could have sparked dry grass behind the ridge near Slick Rock. Or Pennington could be burning, because he didn't have a lick of sense.

"If he's burning trash, I'm calling the sheriff," Eli said.

The thin cloud rose and spread as they watched.

"Make that the fire department." He handed the lead rope to Garcia and ran to the house.

Pennington's phone rang seven times before Eli cut the call and dialed the Spring Valley Fire Department.

"We've got two trucks out now on a lightning strike off Miller's Knob," the dispatcher said. "Is your smoke coming from private property or open range?"

"I can't tell from here," Eli said. "Smoke is clouding up near Slick Rock I'm guessing, one ridge north and east of my place."

"I'll see what I can do, sir. We may have to let it burn if it's not threatening homes."

"If it crosses that ridge, it will be." Eli fumed, knowing what limited resources the county had in this area. If the fire wasn't contained quickly, it could spread into a wildfire, engulfing homes and outbuildings, even livestock.

"Do you have a cell phone number I can reach you on, sir?"

Eli gave the woman his number, ended the call and dialed Laura. Her place bordered Pennington's.

No answer.

He called another rancher to the north to start the domino calls that would alert everyone in the area, then dropped his cell phone in his shirt pocket and hurried to the kitchen window. Laura's car was gone, but the cloud had grown.

Garcia came in the back door. "I will drive the cattle into the lower pasture and open the floodgate."

Eli laid a hand on his friend's shoulder as he passed. "Let's move the sprinklers over here first."

Garcia headed for the west paddock as Eli ran to the barn and brought the four-wheeler around. He backed to the first wheeled sprinkler, hitched up and pulled it to the side yard west of the ranch house. From there the arc would cover the lawns, the house and part of the north pasture.

They repeated the process with the second sprinkler, and set it to cover the barn and outbuildings.

Eli prayed they had enough irrigation water to hold once

Garcia flooded the bottom section. If necessary, they'd pump out the pond.

The cloud had climbed no higher, but it spread wider and spilled south out of the draw that led to Slick Rock. A fire could burn out in the still-tender grass around the mortar bedrock and creek bottom, but if it hit dry grass on the hills it would race up the ridges on either side, pushed by its own wind, and spread in two directions.

"Oh, Lord, help us," he whispered.

Laura's car nosed out from the end of her house. He dialed her number and her voice mail answered.

"This is Eli. You need to get down here. Bring your pets. Pennington's far ridge is burning and if the fire comes over the hill, it could spread your way." He paused, waiting for her to pick up. She didn't. "Hurry."

Again, Pennington didn't answer.

Garcia had already returned to the barn and had two horses saddled. The pungent odor of burning grass tinged the air as the men rode out.

Eli opened the north pasture, then rode south, opening every paddock into the next one. At the alleyways he secured the gates across them so the cattle would stream through to the next section and not turn aside.

Garcia circled around the dry cows in the north pasture and drove them into the neighboring paddock. By the time that first bunch joined the next, the animals sensed the need to move, and funneled easily through the wide gates.

Eli reined in and turned to scan the hills. The cloud had spread. He dialed Laura again. Still no answer. Her five head bunched together at her bottom gate, apparently alerted by the flow of his cattle. Where was she? Why didn't she see what was happening?

He spurred Buddy into a lope, cut around behind the house and reined in at the gate to Laura's bottomland. He opened it and the cows pushed through.

Turning back, he rode for the dairy calves, swung that paddock's bottom gate wide and drove them out. Then he headed for Garcia.

The cattle milled together in the lower section, tension dancing along their backs as they bellowed and jostled. Eli's few horses, including Lady H and her foal, skirted the edges. Garcia knelt at the ditch bank, cranking the wheel that would open the floodgate.

Eli hit redial on his cell phone and whirled Buddy to face Laura's hill. No answer. Squelching an oath to utter a prayer, he dismounted, threw the reins over the top of the fence and ran back to the barn and his truck.

Chapter 21

Laura sat in her car and stared through the windshield. How many days since she'd last checked the mailbox?

The blocky letters suggested a male writer, but she couldn't be sure. She turned the envelope over. The flap was tucked inside, not sealed. An invitation from someone nearby like Lily or Mary? But the envelope looked old.

Just open it.

She slipped a finger inside and tugged at the flap. Pinching a folded edge, she slid out the matching paper.

Nothing written on the outside. No artwork or designs.

Taking a deep breath, she unfolded the note…

I wish you didn't have to go.

Come back again.

Eli Hawthorne III

Stunned by the words, she pressed the letter to her heart and closed her eyes. The years melted away like early morning fog and she saw him again, standing slack-jawed at the pond with his fishing pole. She felt the catch in her voice when she'd said she was leaving.

For how long, he had asked.

Forever, she had said.

Tears gathered on her lashes and fell to her fingers, spreading to wide circles as they spotted the letter.

He'd written. He'd really written. No wonder he asked why she hadn't.

She returned the letter to the envelope, laid it on the dash and drove up the hill.

When did he leave it? Last night? The day before?

As she pulled in next to the house, movement below caught her eye. A cowboy on horseback rode through Eli's west pasture driving the dairy calves through the bottom gate. And then she saw more.

The sprinklers arched over the ranch house and barn. Eli's cow-calf pairs were gone. *Her* cows were gone and the bottom gate stood open.

Her breath stuck in her throat. She opened the car door and smoke-laden air stung her eyes. Rising behind Pennington's house, a wide smoky veil rolled over itself and shifted instantly from veil to churning cloud.

Fire!

She dashed to the house, fumbling with the lock.

"Back," she yelled at the kittens, startling them with her urgency. "No, I mean come." She knelt on one knee. "Come here to me. We have to leave." Calming her voice at their hesitancy, she knew they would pick up on her fear. She didn't have time to lure two frightened animals from beneath her bed.

Grabbing a kitten in each hand, she took them to the laundry room where the dog carrier sat on top of the dryer. She bunched the kittens in an arm, quickly pinched open the mesh door and hustled them inside with their food dish.

She ran outside to a sky white with smoke and fear sparked in her heart.

"Lord, please help us," she prayed, leaving the carrier by the car.

Chica sat forlornly beneath the tree as if about to be abandoned.

"You good girl." Laura squatted to unclip the chain, and the puppy tucked its snout in her lap and whined.

"Come on, Chica, we're going for a ride."

She shut the animals in her car, grateful she'd not put the top down this morning, and ran back inside. Looking around for what she should take, she noticed her bag from the night at Eli's and stuffed in her purse, Bible, laptop, boots, jeans and a shirt. In the kitchen she snatched her cell phone and charger.

The phone registered voice mail. It would have to wait.

She ran back to her bedroom and grabbed the shotgun, then locked the door and hurried to the car. Tiny specs of ash floated in the air. *Lord, help us all.*

Mary! She didn't have the woman's number. She'd have to drive there and warn her—warn everyone if they didn't already know.

"Good girl, Chica," she crooned as she opened the driver's-side door and popped the trunk lever. "Stay."

She laid the shotgun in the shallow trunk and dropped her bag next to it. Slamming the lid, she looked up in time to see the puppy squeeze through the gap between the doorjamb and the nearly closed door.

"Chica! No!"

Frightened by her panicked scream, the pup took off over the crest of the hill and ran toward the bottom pasture.

"Oh, Lord, please!" Laura coughed in the thickening air and glanced over her shoulder. If Pennington's house caught fire, hers could be next.

She pushed the car door all the way closed and went after the puppy.

Eli called again. No answer. Where *was* she? He shoved the accelerator to the floor. Her car nosed out from the hilltop then disappeared from his view as he closed in on the S-curve. He squealed through on his brakes and gunned out the other side. Rocking into the right turn at her road, he climbed the hill as his heart climbed his throat.

Smoke hugged her house like a cloud. He slid to a stop behind the sports car and ran for the French doors.

Locked.

He banged on the door and yelled her name.

Nothing.

No dog. No cats. No Laura.

Running back to the car he saw an animal carrier on the passenger seat. Two black-and-white faces peered at him through the cage door.

"Laura!" His lungs burned in protest as he took a deep breath. "Laura!"

A faint call jerked his head to the left. He listened, called again. She answered from below.

Standing at the edge, he saw her near the bottom, waving. She held the dog under one arm.

"I could use a hand here, Lord," he prayed. "Better yet, a foot."

No time to take the overgrown path that looped down to the bottom. He eased over the edge, leading with his prosthetic foot, giving his full weight to his right leg.

Laura climbed straight up, clutching the dog. At a steeper section, she set the pup down and pulled it along by its collar as she scaled a granite outcropping.

Let it go! he screamed inwardly, knowing the dog would run to safety on its own. He also knew she would never leave it.

An explosion nearly rocked him off balance, and he squatted to look over his shoulder. Black smoke plumed above Pennington's house. He turned back toward Laura. "Hurry!"

She clambered up, reached for him, slipped and started again.

He slid down a few feet, grabbed her hand and pulled. "Give me the dog and keep going."

She handed him the quivering pup and scrambled over the edge.

"Go," he urged, but she waited for him.

He ran for the truck but Laura stopped.

"Come with me," he yelled.

"I'm not leaving the kittens." Terror and determination edged her voice as she opened her car's passenger door.

The fire roared above them, chewing into Pennington's barn and outbuildings. A hot, churning wind rained burning debris.

Eli set the puppy on his pickup seat and slammed the door. Then he bolted to Laura's car where she hefted the carrier. He saw his letter on the dashboard and his heart squeezed.

"Give them to me. I'll put them in the back."

She circled to the driver's side and opened the door. "I have to get my things in the trunk."

"There isn't time." He grabbed her arm and pulled her toward his truck. "Do you have gas cans in your carport?"

She nodded, her eyes wide and wild.

"If they blow, we might not make it off the hill. You can't outrun fire."

He dropped the carrier in the pickup bed and shoved Laura through the passenger door. He stopped and cupped her face with his hands. "I'm sorry. But I'm not going to lose you a second time." Then he slammed the door and ran to the driver's side.

Laura clung to the dog as Eli flew down her crooked lane, frighteningly close to the edge on the curves.

"What about people up the road?" she asked. "Mary Travers and the others?

"They already know. I called them after I called you." He turned his head to see her fully. "Six times. Where *were* you?"

Her dark eyes rounded with fear and tears jeweled along her lashes. "I was reading your letter," she whispered.

Tempted to weep himself, he looked back to the road and concentrated on getting them safely home. And that was exactly where he wanted her—*home* with him.

At the pavement, he slid into a left turn, spraying gravel behind them.

Whirling lights ahead signaled firefighting crews on the

way. At the ranch entrance, he paused as two fire units from the Department of Forestry shot past, followed by a personnel carrier.

He parked at the edge of the bottom pasture and left the dog in the cab. With Laura tucked beneath his arm, he stood next to his truck and watched.

His stomach twisted at the view.

The entire length of the lowest ridge roiled in smoke, and orange flames licked out in the breaks. Laura pressed his side, both arms wrapped around his waist as her house ignited, quivered and crumbled. A cedar tree erupted in a fiery whoosh and the mulberry trees blackened.

When the gasoline cans blew, she jerked and hid her face in his chest.

He encircled her with both arms, grateful that he'd reached her in time.

One DOF truck was already at Pennington's. The other would probably go in from another angle.

Over the top of Laura's head Eli searched for Garcia and found him riding herd from outside the pipe fences. Though agitated, his livestock were secure and safe while the hills burned around them like torches.

Another personnel carrier flew by, and private vehicles poured from the opposite direction—people fleeing to safety as flames spread across the ridge to their secluded homes and acreages beyond. Who knew how long it would be before crews contained the fire?

Laura sobbed against his chest and Eli tightened his hold. The acrid tang of burning rubber floated to them as flames spread beneath the little car and down the hill. An ember shower trailed the very path that he and Laura had climbed.

He laid his cheek against her head. "God, thank You for protecting Laura." He coughed on a sudden surge of emotion. "Thank You."

Frightened bellows cut through his thoughts, but the cries weren't coming from his herd.

Pennington.

He held Laura at arm's length. "I'm going to climb up for a better look."

He swung himself into the pickup bed and climbed to the cab roof. Pennington's scrawny herd pressed into the corner of Laura's new cable and Eli's red pipe fence. He knew barbed wire stretched past his property, farther up the hill. The animals could easily push through it in their frightened state, but they clustered in the southwest corner, the farthest point from the fire. The one point they'd never break through.

If the fire spread downhill through the scrub oak, they'd burn.

He slid to the bed and hopped to the ground. Taking Laura's face in his hands, he ached to kiss her and tell her that he loved her. Instead, he told her his plan.

"Pennington's cattle are trapped and they're not going to move toward the fire to push through his upper stretch of barbed wire."

She wrapped her hands around his. "You're not going up there? Eli, they're not worth your life."

He nearly relented at the fear in her eyes. "I can't let them burn alive. I'll be okay. You stay here and pray."

Quickly he kissed her beautiful lips before issuing one more order. "If the flames spread to the ranch and the irrigated pastures don't stop them, get in the truck and leave."

Still clutching his hands she shook her head.

He tightened his hold. "Promise me. Garcia will ride away, too. He'll open the lower gate and the cattle and horses will run. But you—promise me you'll do as I say."

She reached for his face and pressed her mouth against his. "Promise me you'll come back," she whispered.

"Pray."

Leaving her, he pulled a neckerchief from his back pocket and tied it loosely around his neck and then kicked in to his lopsided gait. He should have driven the four-wheeler and golf cart to safety. Too late now.

"Lord, help me get those cattle out and get back to Laura. Give me your strength."

He jogged into the barn and from the tack room grabbed a pair of wire cutters and shoved them in his back pocket. Then he ran to the tractor shed, hopped on the quad and pulled the neckerchief up over his mouth and nose. Praying he had enough fuel, he headed for the blocked alleyway between his east pastures and the open hillside.

He pushed the gate clear and once past his fence line, shifted gears and raced up the slow rise toward the burning hills. He bounced through dips and around boulders, then angled left toward Pennington's fence line. Four strands ran between older wooden posts in this section, and the fire would easily drop the fence. But it might reach the cattle first.

Eli stopped at the first wire section, cut through the strands on both sides of a post, then bent them all back on either side leaving a wide gap. Returning to the quad, he drove through and turned back down the hillside toward Laura's pasture.

Flying embers threw spot fires ahead of the main blaze, and the encroaching heat pressed through his jeans and shirt.

He slowed as he neared the cattle and stood up, wishing he had Buddy instead. The wide-eyed animals crushed against each other and he waved his hat and hollered as he forced his way between their frightened mass and Laura's smooth cable fence. He had to turn them uphill, and his likelihood of success was minimal.

"Lord, I could use some help here," he prayed. He revved the engine and one bovine reared and swung around, pushing into others behind her. He revved again and two more whirled away. Yelling and revving and waving his hat, he forced them out of the corner, and as a single unit, they trotted along his fence line.

A couple hundred feet and they'd see the opening in the fence. He revved the engine again and hollered. The lead cow saw her chance and broke into a run. The others followed.

Low flames snaked along the hillside and fingered into

a stand of scrub oak. Embers rained down as Eli flew past and the odor of burning straw filled his nostrils. A prick on his head announced the reason and he jerked off his hat. A quarter-size hole had burned through the crown. He tossed it aside and scrubbed his hair.

Following the panicked herd through the gap, he heaved a sigh of relief. He'd made it. Thank God, he'd made it.

The engine choked, sputtered, died. The quad jerked to a stop. Smoke rolled down the hill and swirled around him.

A great calm settled over him as he stepped off the four-wheeler and turned to face the fire. He saw the Humvee, flames licking out from its interior, men screaming where they'd landed on the roadway. One soldier lay crumpled against a low wall. He clutched his face and blood oozed from the bottom of his left leg. The boot and foot missing.

The old has gone, and the new has come.

Eli shook his head at the words and the vision dissipated. He stared at the burning hillside, but saw only oak trees and granite boulders. He coughed and pulled the neckerchief higher across his nose. Then he turned and ran for Laura and the ranch.

Chapter 22

Laura's heart leaped at the sight of Eli hobbling toward her, hatless, covered in ash and drenched in sweat. She flung herself against him, clinging to his hard, trembling body. He held her as if he'd never let go, and she wept in thankfulness for his safety.

By sunset, the ridgeline glowed with orange spot fires. The hills lay draped in sooty black and the distinct aftertaste of scorched grass and charred wood hung thick in the air.

Eli and Garcia moved the sprinklers on foot, struggling with the heavy wheels and hose lines. Stunned by her utter loss, Laura watched her hill from an old garden bench as firefighters soaked the rubble of her family's home, insuring that no smoldering embers reignited. She knew they'd connected to her holding tank—the very reason foothill homeowners were required to have one. Surprised that she had any tears left, she wept again. Chica lay in her lap, evidently accustomed to her mistress's crying.

The Mercedes was gone, its blackened frame a mere pile of

debris. Her pasture had burned to the edges of irrigated Hawthorne land, spreading west to the road and east beyond the new fence. Even Pennington's barren ground had charred. Eli was right. The cattle would have died.

Oak trees stood black-rimmed with leafless lower branches, among them, the Miracle Tree.

Behind her the sounds of moving cattle told her Eli, Garcia and other ranchers who had come to help were driving the animals back to other sections. Garcia pushed the drys into the north pasture beyond the ranch house, but he didn't cut out her five. Why should he? She had nothing for them to graze.

She had nothing period.

Everything Laura had come home to was gone. The tears started anew, and she was glad Eli wasn't there. She'd already soaked his shirt in grief, yet also in gratitude.

Would she have escaped without his help?

"Oh, God, in spite of this loss, I praise You for my life and Eli's."

"Amen."

She turned at the gentle affirmation, set Chica on the grass and stepped into Eli's loving arms. Trying hard to not cry, she laid her cheek against his drumming heart.

He stroked her hair, kissed the top of her head and led her back to the bench. Chica jumped and clawed until Laura scooped her up.

"This old seat may not hold us all," Eli said, his voice heavy with fatigue.

Worry lines scarred his brow and etched the corner of his eye. Laura smoothed them with her fingers, hoping they would someday fade.

The puppy heaved a sigh and dropped its head to its paws. Snuggling under Eli's strong arm, Laura looked again at what was once her home.

"I've lost everything," she said.

With gentle fingers, Eli turned her face toward him. "Have you? Have you really lost everything?"

"I lost my family's home, every possession I had left and my car. I even lost my new boots and any hopes of feeding my cows."

She felt tears pooling again as she whispered, "And I lost your letter."

He wrapped his arms around her with a gentle squeeze. "I'll write you another one, but I can promise it won't say the same thing."

She pulled back and studied his tired, dirty, beautiful face. "Surprise me."

"I plan to."

Exhausted from the day's events, she leaned into him.

"You haven't lost everything," he said. "You have Chica here, and those rascals you call house cats."

She nodded, too tired to answer.

"And you have me."

Fatigue fled as she straightened.

"I do?"

"That's the answer I was looking for."

It took a minute for the play on words to register. But the meaning bloomed in her heart as his lips brushed hers.

"I love you, Laura Bell, you—"

She hushed him with a kiss of her own as a gentle laugh rumbled in his chest.

Epilogue

Laura's new handmade boots showed clearly beneath her pale yellow sundress, and her hair fell softly over her shoulders. She hugged the mixed bouquet against her waist, and tucked her right hand into Garcia's elbow.

He folded a hand over hers. *"Mija,"* he said with a tender smile. "You are more beautiful today than ever before."

"Thank you, *abuelito*. I feel beautiful."

Forty people filled the white-chair rainbow Eli and Garcia had spread around the Miracle Tree, and Pastor Alex Berger stood confidently before them. Right next to Eli, heartbreakingly handsome in his starched Wranglers and white shirt.

Guitar music signaled the beginning of the ceremony and Mary urged Lily ahead. The girl's long cotton dress and meadow-green sash swayed lightly as she scattered white rose pedals over the deep grass aisle dividing the chairs.

Laura gave her friend a final glance.

"Thank you, Mary," she said. "For everything."

Mary had opened her home to Laura after the fire, offering shelter and safety as well as love and acceptance. She blew Laura a kiss and moved back toward the open pasture gate.

A short walk, a sweet kiss on the cheek and Garcia placed her hand in Eli's and took a front-row seat.

Caught up in the beauty around her and the man at her side, Laura heard little of what Berger said to their guests until he mentioned the past.

"We cannot go back and change anything," he said. "We cannot undo what has happened or even return to a certain time or place and find circumstances the same. This is by God's good design and plan."

Berger paused and stepping aside, turned toward the tree.

"We all bear scars of some type," he said. "But with God's healing touch, we survive and grow. By his grace, we carry on."

Facing Eli and Laura again, he continued.

"The unknown is often frightening, but Jesus said He would never leave us alone. Our job is to move forward, into the future, by faith trusting Him."

Eli squeezed the arm she had tucked in his own, and his blue gaze promised a future with the Lord's great love as their guide.

When they exchanged rings, Laura gasped at the diamond-encrusted band Eli slipped on her finger. And in a few brief moments, Berger presented them to their neighbors and friends as Mr. and Mrs. Eli Hawthorne III.

Cowboy hoots and hollers filled the air as they hurried down the aisle and through the pasture gate, running for the barbecue buffet on the east lawn.

Momentarily alone, Eli swept her up in a kiss that sent a tingle all the way down to her boot heels.

"I love you, Laura Bell Hawthorne."

She melted against him, silently thanking God for this new beginning.

Their guests soon joined them and Garcia walked over with a secretive smile.

"My children," he said with great tenderness. "I have a gift for you."

Laura couldn't imagine what more her old friend could give than to give her away.

He strode to the lawn's edge where a long cloth-covered rectangle leaned against the big cottonwood tree. With a bright grin, and a bit of a flourish, he pulled the cloth from a large wooden sign. Two valley oaks were carved into its rich grain, one at either end, and they framed the words, *Rancho Roble Milagro*.

"It's beautiful," Laura said, stooping to finger the deep carving. Hesitant to admit her ignorance, she pondered the name. *Rancho* obviously stood for "ranch," and *Roble* she knew meant "oak." But *milagro?*

Garcia grinned and nodded at Eli.

Lifting her by the hand, he tucked her beneath his arm.

"It's the new name of our ranch. This seemed like the right time to make the change, and what better name than one that means something to all three of us."

Still puzzled, Laura looked to Garcia for a clue.

"Life is a miracle, no?" he said.

And then she knew.

Surprised that her heart had room for any more joy, she turned to the crowd with her arms opened wide.

"Welcome to Miracle Tree Ranch."

* * * * *

HEARTSONG

PRESENTS

Look out for 4 new
Heartsong Presents books next month!

**Every month 4 inspiring faith-filled
romances will be available in stores.**

These contemporary and historical Christian
romances emphasize God's role in every
relationship and reinforce the importance of
faith, hope and love.

REQUEST YOUR FREE BOOKS!

2 FREE CHRISTIAN NOVELS
PLUS 2
FREE
MYSTERY GIFTS

HEARTSONG
PRESENTS

YES! Please send me 2 Free Heartsong Presents novels and my 2 FREE mystery gifts (gifts are worth about $10). After receiving them, if I don't wish to receive any more books I can return the shipping statement marked "cancel." If I don't cancel, I will receive 4 brand-new novels every month and be billed just $4.24 per book in the U.S. and $5.24 per book in Canada. That's a savings of at least 20% off the cover price. It's quite a bargain! Shipping and handling is just 50¢ per book in the U.S. and 75¢ per book in Canada.* I understand that accepting the 2 free books and gifts places me under no obligation to buy anything. I can always return a shipment and cancel at any time. Even if I never buy another book, the two free books and gifts are mine to keep forever.

159/359 HDN FVYK

Name	(PLEASE PRINT)	
Address		Apt. #
City	State	Zip

Signature (if under 18, a parent or guardian must sign)

Mail to the **Harlequin® Reader Service:**
IN U.S.A.: P.O. Box 1867, Buffalo, NY 14240-1867

* Terms and prices subject to change without notice. Prices do not include applicable taxes. Sales tax applicable in N.Y. This offer is limited to one order per household. Not valid for current subscribers to Heartsong Presents books. All orders subject to credit approval. Credit or debit balances in a customer's account(s) may be offset by any other outstanding balance owed by or to the customer. Please allow 4 to 6 weeks for delivery. Offer available while quantities last. Offer valid only in the U.S.

HSPDIR13R